D1806239

Desire
Actually

AFTER OFFICE HOURS, BOOK 1

Jennifer Skully

ISBN: 9781530334872

What's a red-blooded, All-American male supposed to do when his wife divorces him—over email, no less—because she claims he's too *vanilla* in the bedroom?

Get a tutor after office hours, of course.

Enter Jordana Davis, a work colleague who's willing to share the mysterious secrets of what a woman *really* wants. And Grady Masterson is more than willing to listen to every sexy, seductive word of advice Jordana offers.

Everything is fun and games until the sparks start to fly between them. Now, Jordana begins imagining that Grady might be the one who can give her what she really wants—him. If only he wasn't taking lessons from her to win back his wife.

How far would you go to win the one you love?

ACKNOWLEDGMENTS

Thank you to my special network of friends who support me, brainstorm with me, and encourage me: Bella Andre, Shelley Adina, Jenny Andersen, Jackie Yau, Ellen Higuchi, Kate Curran, Ava Bradley, Rosemary Gunn, Laurel Jacobson, and Lloyd Russell. Thank you to Rae Monet for such great covers! Thanks also to Nancy Warren and Linda McGinnis for all their input on the series. A special thank you to Lisa Salvary for her hard work and support and for coming up with the perfect title! As always, my husband is the greatest, helping to make my writing career flourish and my life easier.

CHAPTER ONE

Grady Masterson stared at the email on his monitor. After eight at night, the office was as silent as a stadium once the fans of a losing team had all gone home. Empty and let down. The quiet gave him time to stare at the email longer than he might have if it had arrived in the middle of the day.

He simply couldn't understand it.

He was forty-two years old, a college graduate and Vice President of Business Development for a Silicon Valley start-up that had the potential to make billions. He occupied a corner office on the second floor, with a window and a wood desk instead of plastic cubicle furniture. He owned his own home and came from a large San Francisco Bay Area family who'd never been scandalized by divorce in the ranks—of course, two of his brothers hadn't married yet. He paid his taxes without fudging a single deduction, and he wasn't stupid. At least he'd never thought so until now, when he simply could not comprehend what the email was telling him.

Dear Grady, she'd written. *I'm divorcing you. We're not compatible anymore. Since we don't have kids to worry about, it should be a simple matter. I'll have my lawyer call yours.* She'd signed it as *Your Wife.*

Your wife. As if he was too stupid to recognize the email address. They'd been married fifteen years. Career-oriented, they'd never had children. Right from the beginning, when they were in college, Darlene had told him she wasn't the mothering type. He didn't mind, though his mother had never truly come to terms with the fact that she wouldn't get grandchildren from her first born. He and Darlene had a good marriage. They didn't fight, not about money, not about sex, not even about religion or politics or in-laws.

Then suddenly, without a single warning shot, they weren't compatible and she wanted a divorce.

It defied explanation—or even logic. He understood each individual word. He grasped the overall meaning. What he couldn't fathom was the context, the why.

Swiveling his desk chair, he stared out his window. It wasn't quite dark yet, the late summer sun still streaking the western horizon with the last of the day's rays.

He was more angry than hurt, though he was sure the hurt would come later, after he'd processed the whole thing.

Had she been distant lately? Busy at work, sure, since Darlene was an analyst at a brokerage house. She was always distant when the market was down, which it had been for the last few months. Maybe he'd been distant, too, without even realizing it. A start-up created a huge amount of work and stress, but he'd made time for her. He'd factored that in when he accepted the job eighteen months ago. He usually didn't arrive home until after seven o'clock, or even later. Neither did Darlene. They were happy workaholics. They shared a good meal, usually take-out from one of the nicer restaurants along University Avenue in Palo Alto. They enjoyed a glass of wine together—a new vintage they'd found during a Sunday trip up to Napa in the spring—and tuned into an interesting show on PBS. Or a British mystery. Or… it hadn't really mattered because they both went through email in front of the TV.

He couldn't detect the chink in their marriage. They'd seemed comfortable and well-matched. Maybe they were a little routine, but he was satisfied with that.

The email had left him totally, freaking clueless.

And suddenly he was pissed as hell. It wasn't mere anger. Emotion chewed up his gut like something bad he'd eaten for dinner. It threatened to spew up and out, burning his throat with acid.

He clicked his mouse to force-close his computer. He was done staring at his inbox.

What kind of woman divorces her husband over email? Not the woman he thought he knew, not the woman he'd loved.

Love. The word sent him over the edge, and he grabbed his cell phone off the desk. Jabbing in the pin number to unlock it, he found her name in his favorites and stabbed the icon of her smiling face.

It rang so long he thought she'd let him go to voicemail. Until she said, "Hello." Politely. As if she hadn't even looked at the caller ID.

"What the hell is going on, Darlene?" The sharpness of his voice sliced holes in the quiet office.

"Grady." She paused long enough to communicate her annoyance. "I really don't think we should discuss it over the phone."

"Right. So you can divorce me by email, but we're not allowed to actually talk about it." His fist was so tight on the phone that his knuckles cracked.

"I knew you'd be like this. That's why I sent the email." Because she didn't want to listen. He'd heard the subtext in her tone.

"You can't just make up your mind without even talking about it." He felt his back teeth grinding as he closed his mouth on the words. "Most people would at least try a little counseling. We don't even have any problems."

"That's why we can't do counseling, Grady. Because you won't admit the truth. We've been off for months. Years, in fact. We're little more than roommates. But you're so complacent with the status quo that you don't even notice."

Complacent? He rose and began pacing the office because he couldn't sit still as he listened to her. "Right. We're roommates who have sex once a week. Like clockwork."

"That's what I'm talking about. It's like clockwork. Routine. *Complacent.*" Her voice hissed on the word, like a snake slithering into his comfortable, *complacent* world beneath a rock.

Pulling the phone away from his ear, he stared at her icon a moment. Her snide voice didn't match the smile. It was like she was some other woman. "So this is all about sex?"

"It's not *all* about sex. But I could use a little more

4

variety in the bedroom. It doesn't always have to be Saturday night. It doesn't always have to be step one, step two, step three, we're done. We could be spontaneous. It's all too vanilla."

"So now I'm vanilla, too?" Where did she even come up with that word? "All right, fine. I'll come home and we'll have sex right now. We'll do step three, then step two and step one." He didn't even know what the steps were. Their love life wasn't clockwork. He only chose Saturday because on Friday they were both tired from a long workweek and Sunday night they had to get up early the following morning. And he mixed things up. She'd stopped wanting to kiss, jumping right into things, asking him to put his mouth on other parts of her body instead of on her lips. He'd happily obliged. More than happily for both of them.

She gave a long-suffering sigh, like the mother of a teenager who'd told him to clean up his room for the millionth time. "You really don't get it. When I try to explain what a woman wants, you just don't listen."

"I'm listening now. Tell me what a woman wants."

"It's too late." She snapped out each syllable.

He had to be the calm one. They'd never work things out if they were sniping. "We've been married for fifteen years. We should at least talk face-to-face before we bring in the lawyers. I'm coming home now."

"I'm not *at* home."

"You've already moved out?" This time his teeth ground so hard, he thought he heard one of them chip.

"I've got a hotel room."

It was too freaking weird. "Just like that?"

"I told you've I've been thinking about it."

The idiot lightbulb over his head finally flashed on. "There's someone else, isn't there?"

"Don't be ridiculous." Which translated to: *Yes, there is*.

"How long has it been going on, Darlene?"

"I told you there isn't anyone else." But the softness of a lie had slipped into her tone.

"Tell me."

"I *am* telling you."

"Someone from work?"

"No."

"A client?"

"Of course not."

"Then who?"

"I told you there isn't anyone."

But he knew her. He might not have paid enough attention over the past few months, he might be *complacent*, but with his eyes suddenly wide open—actually, it was his ears—he recalled the subtle differences, clothes ever so slightly sexier, the loss of five pounds, a new tint in her hair.

"I assume he's not vanilla in the bedroom like I supposedly am." His voice snapped like a rubber band.

"Grady, I'm not—"

He knifed through the lie. "You are. But you should know there's not going to be a divorce until we talk. Honestly and openly. Call when you're ready."

He didn't hack at the phone. He simply ended the call with a push of his finger. Then he tossed his cell phone on the desk with a *thunk*.

She was having an affair. He'd claimed he wasn't a stupid man. But he was. He'd missed all the signs. There'd been nights she hadn't come home until ten, but he'd had those late nights himself, for *business*. Over the last few months, the Saturday night intimacy had been at his initiation, and now he wondered if she'd faked her climaxes, too.

He swore, slapped his hand on the back of his chair and rammed it into the desk. Then he grabbed his phone, shoving it into his suit pocket.

They needed to talk. He couldn't leave this hanging. But he didn't even know where she was.

He slammed his office door on the way out. It felt damn good. He relished the sensation as he turned, taking two long strides toward the door

And smacked into a wall that shouldn't have been there. A supple, yielding wall that crumpled to the carpet with a *woomph* of breath and a soft shriek.

Jordana Davis fell on her butt.

"Sorry. Are you okay?" Grady Masterson stretched out a hand to her. With his executive-short dark hair and sexy five o'clock shadow—make that eight o'clock—the guy was totally hot. She'd always thought so. But he looked especially good from her vantage point down on the carpet. She adored big, tall men, and Grady was at least six-two compared to her five foot seven.

"I'm fine. It was my fault." She let him pull her up, her fingers engulfed by his warm, oversize hand. It was most definitely her fault. If she hadn't been eavesdropping on his entire phone conversation, she would have left before he figured out he wasn't alone.

His cheeks turned ruddy, as if he suddenly realized that she'd probably heard everything, right down to the fact that his wife thought he was vanilla in bed.

A wave of heat blushed her face. He had to be wondering why she was here so late. She jerked a thumb over her shoulder, pointing at her computer. "I was polishing Rhonda's Power Point presentation." The excuse was inane. It didn't explain why she'd kept herself hidden. "For the quarterly company meeting tomorrow," she added, which didn't make anything better.

She was executive assistant to the Human Resources VP, whose office was straight across from Grady's. A cubicle wall separated her desk area from Ivy, Grady's assistant. They had identical cubicles, each with a short reception desk in front, desk tops all around, hanging file cabinets, and an opening that faced directly at their respective VP's office. Beyond that was a warren of cubicles housing the Accounting department and a row of offices along the opposite wall while the copy room and conference room flanked the entrance to this upper quadrant of the building.

Grady blinked with eyelashes that were long and dark. "Sorry for startling you when I slammed the door."

She waved away his apology, giggling like a silly schoolgirl. If she hadn't jumped up, he probably would have rushed through like a mini tornado without ever seeing her and saving them both from the embarrassment.

But he'd ended the call, and she'd heard him swear. She'd thought she could slip away without being noticed. What an idiot.

So, was it best to acknowledge what she'd heard or

pretend she'd been engrossed in Rhonda's presentation? That might be a lie too hard to swallow.

He shifted feet. "I didn't hear you out here on your computer."

She had a very quiet keyboard. "I should have been louder."

His dark coffee eyes seemed to glow with tiny slashes of green. Instead of dropping his gaze, he looked at her directly. She counted the long, long seconds of silence. "You heard it all, didn't you." His voice didn't rise into a question but remained flat.

It was less embarrassing to simply nod her answer. She'd heard every dirty detail of his side of the conversation. It wasn't hard to deduce that his wife had sent him a *Dear Grady* email because he was boring in bed and she was having an affair. Or maybe she was having an affair because he was boring in bed. Or… his wife made *her* affair *his* fault by saying he was a bad lover.

His jaw flexed, and he breathed deeply enough to flare his nostrils. She'd never seen Grady Masterson angry. He was big, he was toned—oh yeah, he was toned—but he wasn't a pushy loudmouth. Tonight was the first time she'd heard him raise his voice, his speech clipped and harsh.

"So tell me," he said, his gaze intense enough to create a wash of heat deep inside her. "What do women really want?"

She thought about tossing her purse strap over her shoulder and making a run for it. Or throwing him a bone, something like *We want equal pay for equal work*, or *We want to be taken seriously*. But that wasn't what he needed to hear.

He'd asked sincerely. And since she'd blatantly

eavesdropped on his very personal conversation—because of course it never occurred to her to leave—he deserved an honest answer.

"A woman wants to be desired." Her words came out breathy, sexy. She bit her lip. It wasn't how she'd meant to sound, but there was a change in the atmosphere swirling around them that brought out the huskiness in her voice.

His eyes got darker, the streaks of green receding into the deep cocoa, turning his gaze into something earthy and potent. "How does a man do that?"

"You can't *do* it. You have to *feel* it."

"But how?" He spread his hands, which she realized had been clenched. "Flowers? Chocolate? Fancy dinners?"

"You have to be desperate. You have to be intense." She felt his intensity now, like heat shimmering off concrete.

He shook his head, a short, sharp jerk. "What does that *mean*?"

On a college essay, she'd once gotten the comment that her reasoning needed to be more *compelling*. What the heck did that mean? Same applied here. What did *desperation* and *intensity* mean in concrete terms, especially in regard to the subject matter?

Her breath felt rough in her throat. Then she went for it. "A woman wants to be shoved up against a wall and taken." She swallowed her embarrassment, concentrated on the heat of his earthy gaze. "Tear her clothes off. Like you can't wait one more second to get your hands on her. Just pull up her dress and make her scream with pleasure."

His eyes were all pupil now. She could almost see her reflection in the blackness. "How?" he murmured.

"With your mouth," she whispered. "It's all about

her, *for* her. You don't even get off. You just need to taste her. Right this minute."

There was a scent on the air, his male musk, hers, mingling, pulling them closer.

His lips moved. "That's just lust."

"You can't have the love if you don't have the lust first, because then you're just friends with benefits." That was her preferred modus operandi. Relationships were too fragile and potentially disastrous. She didn't have time for disaster.

Grady stepped closer, invading her personal space. His heat arced into her, surrounded her, seduced her.

"And you've been desired liked that?" he asked so softly his voice was like a feather stroking her erogenous zones.

The question didn't merely invade personal space, it assaulted personal *everything*. She could have told him her answer was theoretical. She could have lied. But in this moment, they were too intimate for lies.

"Yes." She was a desire junkie. "It was the biggest high in the world."

CHAPTER TWO

Jordana licked the gloss on her lips. Grady could almost taste the fruitiness of it. His blood roared in his ears, rushing straight down.

He'd never cheated on his wife, never wanted to, never even thought about it. God help him, though, he was thinking about it now. What had seemed inconceivable in the aftermath of Darlene's divorce email consumed him now. He couldn't even bring his wife's face to mind. Maybe it was the anger flushing away the image, but all he saw was Jordana's lush mouth, and he fell headlong into the deep blue of her eyes, suddenly under the influence of her fast-acting citrusy scent. It seeped in through his pores and took him over. Their proximity revealed the slight rise and fall of her chest with each shallow breath she took. His gaze focused on a lock of her brunette hair against the rapid flutter at her throat. He had the insane urge to bend down and lick her right on that pulse point.

Back up, back up, back up.

The danger signal rang in his head. Taking that first step away was the hardest move he'd ever made.

"I understand." He sounded disgustingly wheezy.

"Do you?" Her voice was still husky, hypnotic.

Hell, yes, he understood intensity, and he was desperate right now. His fingers curled with the need to touch her. His mouth salivated as if she were a savory-sweet piece of meat. His head ached with the fear that he'd lost his mind. Because she wasn't his wife and he shouldn't be feeling any of this.

"Teach me." His voice actually cracked in the middle.

"Teach you what?"

The distance between them shrank. His back was against the wall—physically as well as metaphorically—and he didn't even know how he'd gotten there. "How to make a woman feel desired." He gritted his teeth. "How to make my *wife* feel desired." He stressed the word. It needed stressing. His *wife*. Not Jordana.

The spell around them shifted, space stretched like elastic, and she was no longer within breathing distance. He wasn't sure she ever had been. It might have been his imagination.

"Are you asking me to give you lessons?"

"Pointers. Examples," he said quickly. "Like what you just told me."

They still spoke in hushed voices. Her gaze slid down to his mouth, and a lick of heat passed through him. He told himself that he wanted the theoretical side of desire, but he couldn't help wanting to know more about what turned *her* on.

"Kissing." The word sizzled on her lips.

"Kissing," he repeated. "I can do kissing."

"Not just any old kiss." Her mouth curved in the slightest yet sexiest of smiles. "Wrap your hand gently around my throat. Or cup my face in your palms. Hold me still, devour me with just your lips, nothing else touching, not our bodies, not even our arms. Nothing but the heat between us."

She created an image so tangible that he could taste her on his tongue. His breath came faster, and his pulse beat against the surface of his skin. He needed a demonstration. He wanted...

"You need to watch some chick flicks."

He wasn't sure he'd heard correctly. "Chick flicks?"

Her smile flashed, her hands moved, animation exciting all her facial muscles. "*Bridget Jones's Diary.*"

Good God. *Bridget Jones's Diary*? A man had to have some limits.

She recognized his shock. "When Colin Firth kisses her at the end, it's to die for."

"Then I can just fast forward to the end."

"No-ooo," she exclaimed in two syllables and a wave of her hands. "If you don't see the entire thing, you won't get why the kiss is so hot."

He didn't think he'd get it if he watched the movie five times, but then the sparkle in her pretty blue eyes clued him in. "You're making fun of me."

She would have been completely serious except for the slight twitch of her lips. "Of course not. And there's a reason they're called chick flicks. Because we—" She put a hand to her chest, at which point he thought he might have a heart attack. "—love them. And why? Because they depict what we desire."

"So I can learn everything I need to know from

watching chick flicks?" God forbid.

She laughed. He'd heard her laugh before. After all, he'd seen her five days a week in the nine months since she'd been hired. The lovely sound, however, had never resonated inside him to the point that he missed the next thing she said. "What?" he had to ask.

"Not what, but who. James." As if just the first name said it all, she sighed, affecting a dreamy gaze. "He's an actor. *Becoming Jane*. Boy, can that man kiss. Oh, oh." She fluttered her hands at him. "*Penelope*. He's in that movie, too, and he kisses her the same way. Like he's been thinking about it for months, years even, and suddenly he can't stop himself."

He didn't know who this James person was. "*Becoming Jane. Boy, Can That Man Kiss*. And *Penelope*. I haven't heard of any of those movies." *Becoming Jane* sounded familiar for some obscure reason he couldn't recall, but the other two were a mystery. Darlene had never been the chick-flick type.

Jordana gave him that tinkling laugh again, covering her mouth with her hand. "It's not a movie. I meant that James can really kiss. *Penelope* is sort of a fairy tale. And *Becoming Jane* is about Jane Austen."

"So watching these movies is supposed to teach me how to kiss?"

She shrugged, a sexy little shimmy that seemed to twist through her whole body. She'd laughed, shrugged, and done all those things in front of him before, he was sure, but her gestures had never elicited a response like this. He'd never even actively noticed. It had all been subliminal. But somehow, from the moment she'd told him exactly how to make her melt with desire, he couldn't *stop* noticing.

"It's a start," she said. "But it isn't just the kiss. It's all the stuff leading up to the kiss. The dance. The furtive looks. The subtext. The innuendo." She rolled her eyes like a teenage girl, and he was suddenly aware of their twelve-year age difference. "You're married," she added. "You must have done the dance at some point."

"I've been married for fifteen years, and we dated for five years before that." They'd both thought it was reasonable to get their careers going strong before getting married. "It's been a long time."

"That's your problem then. You've forgotten. You need reminding."

Jordana had certainly reminded his body of something.

She gasped. And that did more strange things to him. "You've got to watch *Castle*. I think it takes them something like five seasons of that show to finally get there." In her excitement, she bounced a couple of times on the toes of her high-heeled shoes. "And *Buffy the Vampire Slayer*. Not the Angel thing, but Spike."

He didn't have a clue what she was talking about. Except that *Buffy the Vampire Slayer* was some sort of teenage angst show about vampires… and teenage girls.

Sighing exaggeratedly, she caressed him with another dreamy smile. "The whole secret love-hate relationship is so sexy. It's totally what women want. We want the fantasy. That we're the only one and you'll do anything to have us."

That dreamy smile was getting to him, making his heart kick and his palms sweat. Not to mention other things. But a man truly did need to have his limits. "No self-respecting man of forty-two watches chick flicks and *Buffy the Vampire Slayer*."

She put her hands behind her back and took one step too close to him. He couldn't think when she was this close. Or rather, he thought too much about things he shouldn't even allow into his married brain. "Are you saying," she said, deadly soft, "that you're not willing to do anything, *absolutely* anything, to get your wife back?"

The challenge jerked him out of the sexual daze he'd fallen into. Darlene had left him and not five minutes later, he was entertaining inappropriate thoughts about another woman. A much younger woman with gorgeous blue eyes and sexy, messy, silky dark chestnut hair and… other attributes he had no right speculating about. And she'd just voiced the only question that really mattered: Was he willing to do absolutely anything to get Darlene back?

"You're angry right now."

Her remark brought her face into focus again. She'd heard his side of the phone argument, and he was pretty damn sure he'd revealed everything in the heat of the moment. "You could say that." He could feel his teeth start to grind again.

"But do you really want to throw away fifteen years of marriage?"

In his anger, yes. If Darlene was cheating on him, definitely. But if he was completely honest, did she bear the entire blame? Or had he simply dug a hole so deep in the sand that it covered not only his head, but sucked in his whole body, too? He'd been comfortable with their life, but he'd never asked if she was. He'd taken everything for granted. He was complacent, just as Darlene had claimed. It didn't justify cheating or excuse divorce by email, but did he want their marriage to be over without even a fight? "I don't know."

He was answering Jordana. He was answering himself.

"So show her what she thinks she's been missing. It certainly couldn't hurt."

He tried to lighten the moment. "It could if anyone found out I turned into a chick-flick addict."

Her mouth in a half smile, she drew her fingers across her lips. "Totally sealed."

He sighed, trying to sound dramatic. "All right, you win. But I don't have Netflix, and I'm not even sure where there's a video store." In the age of mail-order DVDs and streaming, most of the video stores had gone out of business.

She beamed in high wattage. "You're in luck. I have them all on DVD and I'll let you borrow them."

"Wonderful," he said dryly.

"And for every movie you watch, I'll give you a gold star."

"Great." He almost groaned. "I'll be the teacher's pet."

She clapped her hands. "Doris Day and Clark Gable in *Teacher's Pet*. I forgot to mention all the classics you should watch, too. *Gentlemen Prefer Blondes*. *Pillow Talk*. *An Affair to Remember*. They're fabulous." She cocked her head. "Although the kisses aren't quite the same as you see in movies today." Then she added with huge affectation, "Oh my gosh, we can't forget *Love Actually*. Yeah, *Love Actually* is totally perfect." She gave him a cheeky smile. "So many chick flicks, so little time."

What the hell had he gotten himself into?

The next morning, preparations for the quarterly company meeting commandeered everyone's focus. Rhonda wasn't satisfied with the changes Jordana had made to her presentation, despite the fact that they were exactly what she'd asked for. Jordana was also in charge of making sure the cafeteria was converted into a makeshift auditorium with enough chairs, bottles of water, the right AV equipment, that all the VPs had their updated agenda, and on and on.

She didn't have a moment to pass over the DVDs she'd brought for Grady. She hadn't stopped thinking about last night. He'd made her laugh, especially with his obvious horror at having to watch chick flicks. Sometimes attraction was like a bolt of lightning the first time you saw a man, that chemical thing that tripped all your nerve endings. Other times it was slow-growing, until one day you realized your feelings for a guy had been percolating inside you. This was somewhere between the two, where lightning struck and suddenly made her see Grady Masterson as far more than the VP across the hall.

Of course, he was married, even if his wife had just dumped him. And Jordana stuck strictly to single men.

Over the years, she'd been absorbed by her career, and dating had never been top priority. Men tended to get in the way, wanting you to divide your attention between your work and their needs. That was one of the reasons she didn't go in for long-term relationships. Besides, keeping everything short-term meant there was less chance of being hurt or getting dumped. She also wasn't ashamed to admit she liked hot, fast, and intense, something with a bit of an illicit nature, like sneaking away at lunch for a quickie. She preferred the high of lust versus the pressure of a relationship, at least until she'd achieved her career goals. That didn't mean she would *never* think about marriage. She saw herself as a mother eventually, and having her dad run off when she was only three—no calls to check on her, no letters, not even a card on her birthday—had taught her that a child needed both parents. So she'd get married at some point in the future, but at thirty years old, there was plenty of time ahead of her for all that.

Her career came first right now, and she'd fallen behind right out of the gate. It took her three years to finish junior college because she was working at the same time. Same with university. She'd had a scholarship to San Francisco State, but she'd worked as well and couldn't handle a full load of classes every term, so she'd graduated later than planned.

"Hello. Earth to Jordana."

Jordana nearly fell off her high heels. Squatting on the floor to arrange bottles of water and cans of soda in the ice filling the metal tubs, she hadn't even heard Rhonda crossing the floor in her sensible, rubber-soled shoes.

"I asked if you'd loaded my presentation on the laptop. And you were a million miles away."

Jordana pushed herself up from her crouch in the front of the drink tubs. "Yes, Rhonda."

To put it diplomatically, Rhonda was a micromanager, with occasional bursts of outrage she pretended hadn't happened. That trait made it doubly odd for her to run the quarterly leadership workshops. Rhonda accentuated her matronly appearance by favoring staid business suits and a short hairstyle that added an unnecessary sense of plumpness to her face. She refused to dye the gray out of her hair, saying that as a woman in a man's world, she wouldn't use her sex appeal to her advantage. What sex appeal? Jordana hadn't asked that obvious question in the nine months she'd been Rhonda's assistant. She circumvented the micromanaging with politeness and ignored the outbursts. She didn't work in Human Resources for nothing, after all.

"You can look it over and make sure everything is the way you want it." Jordana had loaded the PowerPoint presentations. All the speaker had to do was a push a button to move through their slides. She tapped a few keys, and Rhonda's headcount numbers appeared. Staff had grown by 20 percent over the last quarter, and all the new hires were in Manufacturing, which was exactly where they should be. After a long stint of R&D, the company was scheduled to begin shipping product by the first of the year, and they'd received a large influx of cash from a group of venture capitalists in order to make that happen.

Rhonda plodded through every slide, making more changes Jordana knew she'd have to fix before the meeting. "Are you sure about this number?"

"I checked it the first time you asked me, Rhonda." Jordana forgave the micromanaging, but she still let her boss know she was doing it. Again.

"Oh yes. I forgot." Rhonda allowed her the reminder. She'd never gone off on Jordana, maybe because Jordana called her on the small managerial infractions.

Rhonda Clark wasn't the best boss or the best

example to follow, but she knew her stuff, and Jordana soaked up knowledge like a sponge. She wanted the VP spot, not Rhonda's specifically, but something in a fast-growing, dynamic company. That's why she'd gone for a start-up, because she wanted training in everything to do with the HR field. Since college, she'd worked in two conglomerates, and while the experiences had been good—she'd even worked in Payroll for a while to familiarize herself with that technical area—overall, she'd been slotted into one tiny area of expertise, never getting the big picture. That wasn't for her. She had too much to catch up on to remain narrowly focused. If she wanted the top job, she had to be proficient in every aspect.

Training aside, with a start-up, there was the added benefit of stock options when the company went public.

While Rhonda went through her presentation, Jordana returned to stacking drinks in the tubs. Even organizing events like this, she considered a skill to be learned. The meeting could totally suck, and she'd been to plenty of yawners like that. There was an art to making sure the assembly listened to every word.

Of course, there wasn't much she could do about Rhonda's actual performance.

"Oops," Rhonda said loudly.

"What did you do?" Jordana didn't panic. Yet. Rhonda wasn't the most technically savvy, but she couldn't do that much damage in five minutes.

"All I did was tap a key and it went away." Rhonda stared bewildered at what was now a blank screen rather than her document.

"You probably just closed the file." Jordana had merged all the presentations into one file so that the change in speaker was seamless.

The file, however, wasn't in the directory. She checked the trash, just in case. She did a search. Nothing.

"Only you, Rhonda. You hit one key, that's all?"

"I don't know." Rhonda made a face. "This pop-up thingie appeared, and I clicked *Yes* to get rid of it."

"Hmm." The file simply wasn't on the company server. Somehow Rhonda had trashed it, then deleted it out of the trash, too—if that was even possible without knowing you were doing it. Jordana didn't scream. Everything was backed up on her computer. She had time to fix it. "I'll run upstairs for a minute."

"But we have to start in a minute," Rhonda whined.

Not that Jordana was an eye-roller, but seriously. "The room's empty, Rhonda. We've got time to fix it."

"But…"

There were a lot of things Jordana *didn't* want to learn from Rhonda. Like being a worrier and a nitpicker. "I'll be back."

The cafeteria door opened with the first arrivals. The warehouse contingent came for the free drinks. Jordana squeezed past them and headed across the lobby to the stairs, her heels clicking on the tile floor. She pushed upstairs against the flow of accountants coming down.

The building was divided in two, the cafeteria and a testing facility downstairs on either side of the lobby. Upstairs was Marketing, Customer Service, and the CEO's office on one side, Accounting, HR, and Grady's office on the other side. The factory, warehouse, and R&D were in the bigger building across the street. She had time. It would take at least five minutes for everyone to arrive and get seated.

After swiping her card key for the outer door, Jordana skirted the outside of the Accounting bullpen. She turned the corner into her cubicle next to Rhonda's office. Ivy, Grady's assistant, had already left for the meeting, and Grady's office was empty, too.

She smiled thinking of the bag of DVDs she'd dump on him after the meeting. Or maybe she should wait until after office hours.

Jordana punched in her password for her screensaver. In a matter of seconds, she had the file copied onto a flash drive. That way, if anything else went wrong during the meeting, she could quickly transfer.

Tucking the flash into the palm of her hand, she glanced at her watch. Almost show time. Rhonda was probably hyperventilating and clutching her chest by now. It wasn't as if their CEO couldn't talk off the cuff for a few minutes. Brett Baker didn't require slides to do his rah-rah bit.

She was moving fast as she rounded the corner, heading for the door to the upstairs landing.

And smashed right into a hard chest.

He grabbed her shoulders to steady her. She knew that chest. Her face buried against it, she knew that scent, too. Manly soap and tall, sexy man.

"We have to stop running into each other like this," Grady said.

She liked the hint of laughter in his voice. And his hands on her shoulders. And her face in his chest. It was enough to make her forget about the flash drive.

"You're finally getting it." She kept her words soft, a little seductive.

He stepped back, and after a beat longer than

necessary, dropped his hands. "Getting what?"

"What women want."

"Really?" His tone was slightly mystified, his head tilted to the left. "How?"

"That was extremely sexy. Putting your hands on me to keep me steady. Talking before you let me go. Drawing out the moment."

His mouth lifted at one corner. "Was I supposed to let you fall?"

"If I'd bumped into Rhonda, I'm pretty sure she wouldn't have held me up. And you wouldn't have done it if you'd crashed into Brett."

A full-throated laugh burst out of him. "You've got me there."

"So that means you're learning."

He regarded her with those delicious hot chocolate eyes of his. "I wouldn't have done it for Rhonda either."

"See." Something tingled low inside her. "You really are catching on."

His raised brow accentuated a naughty, crooked smile. "But what if you thought I was sexually harassing you?"

She heard the ticking of her internal clock. She even thought she could hear steam venting out of Rhonda's ears. But she couldn't move. This was way too much fun. "You knew I wouldn't. Especially after our conversation last night. Lesson number two, learn when a woman doesn't want anything from you at all. And steer clear."

"I'm still not sure how I'll know." This close, he seemed bigger, taller. And totally sexy in his white shirt and tie.

"When a woman brings you a big bag of chick flicks,

you just know which way it is."

"You brought me presents." He grimaced. "Thank you so much. My weekend will be the envy of every red-blooded American male."

She winked. "I'll let you slip in a pre-season football game as well."

"I'm afraid I only watch the Super Bowl."

Jordana gaped at him. "That's sacrilege."

"Even un-American," he agreed with a straight face and a slight curve of his mouth. "I prefer Indy car races."

She imagined the thunder of the engines pounding in her chest. It was almost sexual. She felt her body swaying into him.

Jordana's internal alarm was now shrieking, and everything she'd ignored for the last few minutes came charging back. The meeting. The flash drive with all the presentations. Rhonda's wrath.

Grady made her forget all her important duties. And that could be very dangerous.

CHAPTER THREE

It was a dangerous game. Grady couldn't stop playing.

On Friday after the company meeting, Jordana had dropped the bag of DVDs on his desk. Then Monday morning, she'd asked him which ones he'd watched.

"*The Thomas Crown Affair*," he told her. He'd shuddered when he'd read the title of *Pretty in Pink*, another of the movies in the bag, teenage angst stuff. And *Love Actually*? Sure, she thought it was perfect, but romance vignettes all tied up in a Christmas bow? Desire or not, he *actually* couldn't stomach it.

Hip cocked, she'd mock glared at him. "That's all you watched?"

It was the only one he could force himself to put in the player. It turned out to be quite good, not a chick flick at all. "The chess game was extremely sexy."

She'd almost let her humor get the better of her, a smile twitching at the corners of her mouth. "Agreed. But there wasn't one stand-out kiss like in *Bridget Jones's Diary*

27

or *Penelope*."

"Then why did you put the DVD in the bag?" he'd asked reasonably.

Her answer was simply to growl. If he could have kept her in his office longer, he would have. But she was at Rhonda's beck and call for something that morning. The woman kept Jordana so busy that he sometimes gave his assistant Ivy on loan for projects that didn't involve confidential employee information.

On Tuesday when Jordana asked, he'd said he had to work late and hadn't had time for a movie. He didn't want to learn from movies. He imagined Jordana giving him hands-on lessons. Or was that lips-on?

Yes, it was dangerous. Every thought seemed to lead back to Jordana. Instead of leading back to his wife.

Disgusted with him, Jordana ordered him to return the cache of DVDs.

The following morning—while Ivy was in the copy room and Rhonda was nowhere to be seen—Grady handed them over, feeling a mixed sense of relief and disappointment. Until Jordana pointed her finger at him, eyes narrowed, and said, "Conference room. Seven o'clock tonight. Be there or be square. I brought popcorn, too."

"So it's not homework anymore?" Thank God.

"I decided that, in all good conscience, it wasn't fair to make you watch your first chick flick all by yourself. In addition, it requires blow-by-blow commentary to make sure you really get it."

"Blow-by-blow?" He swore he felt his eyes widen involuntarily.

"Don't forget the word *commentary* in there."

"Believe me, I won't forget a thing." He couldn't get

Jordana out of his mind.

By seven o'clock that evening the building was empty. Jordana used the DVD player in the conference room, which was hooked up to a large flat screen monitor that did double duty for presentations, Skype calls, and webinars. Microwave popcorn scented the air. Grady was eating his fair share of it. Seated next to each other in two chairs along the wall, they held the bowl between them.

Not that he would admit it aloud lest he should lose his membership to the men's club, but Bridget Jones had an extremely humorous outlook on life. The movie had its chick-flick elements, but it was also funny. And sexy. When Bridget and her boss had exchanged titillating emails, Grady saw the possibilities. He wondered how Jordana would react to a naughty email during the workday. Or a sext. He knew what phone sexting was, he'd just never done it. He wondered how Darlene would have reacted. But really, how did you sext with a woman you'd been married to for fifteen years?

That's your problem, Grady.

He heard Jordana's voice in his ear. He should have thought of sexting. It might have been that *something different* Darlene was looking for. She probably sexted with her lover.

Red-hot anger spiked through him, sucking up all his amusement like a vacuum. He hadn't called Darlene. He hadn't lain awake for hours thinking about losing her. Maybe there was something wrong with him because he'd slept just fine all alone on his side of the bed. Still, he'd woken each morning with a sharp jab of anger in his side, and he felt it stab again at random moments during the day when he let his guard down long enough for an image of

Darlene with another man to slip in.

"Have you ever done that?" With his wife still haunting his thoughts, his voice was sharper and louder than he'd intended.

A piece of popcorn halfway to her lips, Jordana turned her head. "Done what?"

"Sent sexy emails. Or texts. Sexting." He waved a hand at the screen. "Like the whole thing about the little skirt."

Her smile was slow and seductive. It lit up her eyes. She paused the movie, pulled the bowl of popcorn into her lap, and leaned an elbow on the chair arm, propping her chin on her fist. "Yes. It can be very exciting."

"During the day at work?"

She nodded her head. "Uh-huh." Her mouth seemed extraordinarily lush and kissable.

Grady forgot all about his wife. Again. That was a good thing. Or a very bad thing. "Do you get explicit?" His heart thumped harder against the wall of his chest.

"Well," she drew out the word. "This is how I like it. The man gets explicit." She chewed the edge of her lip a moment, and he couldn't take his eyes off her mouth. "Not nasty but seductive and classy." She tipped her chin down and gazed at him through her lashes. "Dirty but not gross."

"Like what?" His mouth went dry waiting for her response.

"Hmm." She gave it long consideration, her eyes going a little dreamy. "Maybe he says he'd like to drag my panties off with his teeth, then kiss me everywhere."

His face flushed. He actually felt the wave of heat rise up his neck and into his cheeks. God help him, something else was rising, too. "That sounds—" His voice cracked. "—interesting." He tried not to look like he was gulping air. "What else?"

"Maybe he says that seeing me in my tight Lycra top makes him want to bury his face between my breasts."

"Uh-huh." He was definitely finding it difficult to breathe.

"So you see? Explicit and even dirty, but never crass. No mention of *holes*—" He barely suppressed a laugh at her wrinkled nose. "—or crude body parts. Not that I mind the mention of body parts. Just no locker room words."

He'd heard crude locker room talk. It was amazing that his generation was just as bad as the younger.

Maybe some things, though, were all about age. Jordana was unique, straightforward. She said things he could never have imagined Darlene saying out loud. At least not when they were first dating. It was possible he wasn't the only vanilla partner in his marriage, at least compared to Jordana.

"The same goes for phone sex." As if it were the end of the discussion, Jordana put the popcorn bowl back on the chair arm between them.

"Phone sex?" he echoed. Of course he knew what it was, but he'd always envisioned dirty old men sitting in the dark calling 999 numbers late at night.

She laughed. "You really do need to get out more often. Didn't you ever go on business trips and call your wife at night?"

"I called her." His voice was dry, just the way those phone calls had been.

She heaved a sigh and shook her head in mock

disgust. "But you never got explicit."

He wagged his head slowly, sadly. "Neither crass nor sexy, not even dirty."

"I'm so sorry for you."

"I supposed I've missed out on a lot."

"Totally."

He needed lessons, more of them, many more. And Jordana began teaching by starting the movie again and forcing him to watch.

Finally she grabbed his arm, squeezing. "This is the best part."

"The kiss?"

"Bridget on the fire pole."

Good God, Bridget on the fire pole. He laughed out loud.

Jordana nudged him with her elbow, almost upsetting the popcorn. "I knew you'd laugh."

"It's the first time I have."

She pursed her lips, narrowed her eyes, and shook her head sadly. "I had no idea you were such a liar."

Yes, he was a liar because he'd laughed a lot, especially at the tarts and vicars party. Jordana was right, though, Bridget on the fire pole was not to be missed. And as the scenes ticked by, his sides began to hurt with the laughter he let out, and the laughter he tried to keep in. He thoroughly enjoyed Jordana, too, even more than the movie, the way she laughed, with her whole body and every muscle in her face. She licked the butter off her fingers, and something tightened inside him. She licked her lips, and everything got worse. Oh yeah, he was enjoying Jordana. Way too much. His wife had left him less than a week ago, and he'd stopped thinking about her. There had to be something wrong with him.

Then Jordana clutched his arm again, her fingers warm, her skin soft, her scent citrusy yet salty with buttery popcorn.

"Okay, here comes the kiss," she whispered, seducing him. "Pay close attention to every nuance."

Bridget was running half naked down a snowy street. There was some dialogue, which might have been silly but was also kind of sexy. Then the kiss.

Grady couldn't help himself. He looked at Jordana, his heart somersaulting inside him. Her slightly parted lips were plump and beckoning. His tongue tingled with her buttery flavor as if he'd actually tasted her.

"You're not watching," she singsonged without even turning her head.

While the kiss was decent enough, it didn't make him hot. It was Bridget Jones, not Jordana. But with her hand on his arm, he couldn't help imagining her instead of the actress.

Camera draws back, music starts playing, snow keeps falling, couple keeps kissing.

"What did you think?" She gave him an expectant, wide-eyed look.

What he thought was that he needed to do something, not just watch. But he couldn't do *something* with Jordana. He needed to focus on his reasons for being here. His wife. His marriage. Forget the anger. After all, he didn't know for sure that Darlene was cheating.

"I think I can do it." If he'd been completely sure, he'd have dropped the word *think*.

She beamed at him with all her perfect white teeth. And full lips. And pretty eyes.

Hell, he needed to stop looking at her like she was a mint chocolate he wanted to devour.

"So now you get a second chance to fulfill your original assignment." She delved into the bag beside her chair. "Start with *Penelope* and *Becoming Jane*." She shoved the DVDs at him. "At the end of each movie, pay particular attention to the way James practically launches himself at Penelope and Jane. And watch Season Six of *Buffy the Vampire Slayer*. The whole relationship with Spike. And don't forget *Love Actually*."

He'd *actually* like to forget it. "Do I really have to watch these by myself?"

"That's what homework is. I got you started. You have to do the rest yourself." Rolling out of the chair, she retrieved the movie from the player. Her high heels and her long legs spiked deep into his psyche.

She'd certainly gotten him started.

Turning, she smiled. Then clapped her hands. "Chop-chop. You can fit in another movie tonight if you hurry home."

He didn't want to stand. She might see the effect she had on him. Jordana herself, *not* the movie kiss.

Didn't she feel any of it?

The answer was obviously no, and that was the way it should be. He was still married, whatever Darlene had done. But watching sexy movies with a beautiful woman who liked emails about a man dragging her panties off with his teeth, hell, any red-blooded male would have a reaction.

"Do I have to watch both movies in their entirety?"

She crossed her arms. He thought of the tight Lycra tops she liked. Who had sent her those emails? And how far had she gone with the man?

He almost missed what she was saying. "You can fast-forward through the whole thing if you promise to watch the kiss at least five times. In *both* movies."

He was too old to go crazy thinking about what she'd done with her lovers. At least that's what he told himself. "*Five* times?"

Her lips creased in a broad smile. "Either that," she paused for drama, "or you have to watch the whole movie."

"On one condition."

Her chest expanded with a breath and held. Then she said, "What?"

"Do not ever tell anyone I watched *Bridget Jones's Diary.*" That wasn't the condition he wanted to put on it. Not at all.

She laughed. "Deal."

He wondered just how much more he'd get than he'd bargained for. Or how much more he'd beg to have.

She needed a lesson plan. Jordana was really getting into the idea of playing teacher to Grady, mulling it over after last evening's movie in the conference room. Her morning had been busy, as if people churned their grievances overnight, then did a data dump on her desk first thing. She would rather be planning sex classes—*desire* classes would be a better description—for Grady.

And as terrible as it was to use up worktime, that's what she'd done all day, in spare moments or when she was doing rote tasks. She'd planned for Grady. First lesson, kissing in movies. Done. Second lesson? There was definitely sexting and phone sex. The man's repertoire was woefully lacking, though she couldn't blame him. He'd been married a long time, after all. Did they even have texting and email when he was in college? It was like the dark ages. Not that she thought of Grady as old. He was totally hot.

So, kissing, sexting, and phone sex. Then, of course, there was sexual tension, desire building, sexy banter, longing looks, sexual touching disguised as something else. Honestly, she didn't have a clue how to describe all that. It just happened.

Like the way Grady had put his hands on her shoulders to steady her when she'd run into him just before the company meeting, holding her far longer than appropriate or necessary. There was also the way he focused on her lips when he talked to her. She couldn't remember his gaze locking on her mouth like that, not before she'd overheard that conversation with his wife. And when she told him how hot it was for a man to simply shove her up against a wall and lift her skirt, the steam had practically vaporized right off his skin. Of course, there was sitting next to him with all the sexual content in *Bridget Jones's Diary*, especially during that to-die-for kiss. She couldn't even look at him, her mind consumed with thoughts of his lips on her and his mouth whispering those sexy words. Now *that* was sexual tension. But how could she describe it? She certainly couldn't say, *This is how I feel about you.* The lessons were supposed to be about his wife. Who *didn't* deserve him. But Jordana wasn't one to judge when she'd eavesdropped on only one side of the conversation.

Maybe her attitudes about sex were too progressive. When had friends with benefits become normal and accepted? What did Grady really think of her? Of course, it didn't matter. She wasn't ashamed of who she was or the sexy things she'd done. She actually felt empowered. She wasn't bogged down with looking for a relationship so she was immune to getting hurt. She was free. And she was just the kind of woman who could teach Grady how to let go of his inhibitions.

Besides, she hadn't done any fooling around since she'd started this job. She'd carried on that casual friends-with-benefits liaison with the guy from her previous company, but that had ended six months ago. She was ripe for a sexy flirtation. Of course, there were limits to this interlude with Grady—like no touching since she was *only* teaching him—but that was a good thing. The limits were also a safeguard against getting caught. She might be ripe for flirting—and she was definitely enjoying this flirtation way too much to give it up—but she had to be careful about her job.

"I need this first thing tomorrow morning." Rhonda tossed a scribble-filled sheet of lined paper on Jordana's desk.

Jordana examined the note. It was now almost five o'clock, and everyone else had started shutting down their computers. With all that planning occupying her mind— and she was a very good multitasker—the day had flashed by. Of course, Rhonda's request meant creating a special report in the HR database. It was a doable task, but she'd have to work late. Rhonda didn't apologize for throwing the request at her so close to the end of the day.

And Jordana wasn't bothered one tiny bit. "Sure thing, Rhonda. No problem." *Thank you very much for the excuse to work late in an office empty of everyone except Grady Masterson.*

It was so much better as well as less risky—even though the risk made it all the more sexy—to flirt *after* office hours.

Hmm, lesson plan. She knew just where to start.

Rhonda left at five sharp. Ivy followed her out two minutes later. Ivy was a single mom and never stayed late. Her daughter was her priority, and Jordana admired that. By five-thirty, Rhonda's report was completed and the accounting cubicles were silent. Grady's office door, however, was still open. She'd seen him in and out all day. He'd said hello, and he'd looked. Long, lingering looks every time he passed. Of course, she was the only one who would interpret them that way. Someone else might imagine he was simply glowering at her. Sometimes he smiled, a secret, sexy smile that blasted her temperature from normal to overheated.

She dialed his office landline and heard his voice in duplicate, on the phone and echoing from his office. "Yes?"

"What's your cell phone number?"

He hesitated only a few seconds before reciting it.

"Thank you. Bye." She hung up and typed a text. She could have sent an email, but the company servers backed up every night, and she didn't want any possibility of there being a trace of what they were doing. She wanted this job, and really, for an HR employee to be playing sex games was, in a word she'd already used for herself, *dangerous*.

Still, she couldn't help herself. Jordana loved sex.

Seriously, she couldn't live without it. In today's world, why shouldn't a woman be like a man? She didn't hurt anyone, had never run out on a guy or abandoned him, and she'd never neglected her job. She had the *right* to play the field, sow her wild oats, or any other cliché that came to mind. Not that she intended to sow any oats with Grady, except verbally, since he was married and this was all about getting his wife back. She was certainly going to make it fun, though.

Her thumbs flew over her phone's keyboard. *Sexting 101, good for email and texting. Your first assignment, write a naughty text to me.*

She had to admit to a slight bump in her pulse rate, a heat in her blood, and a tingle of anticipation. Still, she'd make it as safe as possible for the two of them by deleting all the texts when they were done. And she'd have Grady do the same. A few moments later, her phone double beeped, signaling a text.

What should I say?

Jordana shook her head sadly. The man had so much to learn. *If you were right here in front of me, you would see me rolling my eyes at you. Just type something.*

She had no idea what he'd come back with.

Tell me the most erotic thing you've ever done.

That was unexpected. She hadn't figured he'd turn it back on her. But as far as sexting, it was actually quite good. Get the woman to talk about herself, to tell you what she loves.

She realized she should have done things on email because texting the whole thing was a pain. Still, her own story notched her thermostat up another few degrees, not just the memory but also sharing such an intimate moment with Grady.

A colleague and I were working on a project together over several days, using the same computer, hunched over the same keyboard.

She sent that, waited for the next beep of her phone.

This happened during office hours?

She felt breathless, as if they were having a face-to-face conversation.

Oh yeah. It was summertime and I was wearing a low-cut lacy sleeveless vest.

I'm getting hot just imagining it.

So was she. She continued typing. *The air conditioning was on too high and I was shivering.*

Texting was usually truncated words and acronyms, but for effect, Jordana typed everything out, accepting her smart phone's suggestions to make it faster.

Was this a male colleague you were working with?

She laughed out loud and typed. *Yes. My nipples were hard little buds in that vest.*

I'm sure they were and he couldn't take his eyes off them.

Exactly. All that sexual tension bubbling between us.

I can feel it.

So could she.

He asked if I was cold and I told him yes. She remembered it vividly and thought of Grady in his office staring at her words. The combination was even more erotic than that day in front of her computer.

He touched you?

I touched him.

Even better.

I put my hand on his arm to let him feel how cold I was.

Just his arm?

That was enough.

I'm dying over here. Don't keep me in suspense.

She was dying, too, caught in both the memory and this moment with Grady.

He said he'd warm me up then he grabbed my hand and stuck it between his legs.

The shock of what he'd done had immobilized her. With her heart beating so hard she could feel it against her eardrums, she typed another message before Grady even answered.

I can't remember how many seconds I sat there with my hand between his clenched thighs. Long seconds in which anyone could have walked by the cubicle we were seated in. The heatwave coming off him actually singed my skin.

Did you have sex with him?

She'd been mindless with desire. He'd wanted her just as badly, looking at her mouth, then her hard nipples against the lacy vest. She was a desire junkie, and she couldn't have resisted even if she'd wanted to.

Yes. That very day.

Did you spend the night with him?

No. I don't do overnight stays with anyone. This was during lunch. In his truck out on some deserted road he found.

Grady's reply was immediate, without spaces or punctuation. *Imhard*

I'm wet. Then she put her hands to her face, her skin blazing beneath her fingertips.

He was suddenly there on the other side of her reception desk. His nostrils flared as he breathed hard and fast. She was still cupping her cheeks as he towered above her, and that, too, did something to her insides. She focused on his eyes, which were dark beyond desire.

"You get an A plus," she whispered.

"You did all the work."

"It doesn't matter. You produced the desired effect."

He blinked, slowly, almost as if he were lowering his gaze to take in every inch of her. "And that is?"

She held out her wrists. "Racing pulse." She put her fingers to her face. "Flushed cheeks." And finally, her palm against her chest just above the scooped neck of her top. "Fast breathing."

"What else?" His eyes were so hot, they burned her up.

She held his gaze for three rapid beats of her heart. "Maybe we should leave that description for Phone Sex One-oh-one."

CHAPTER FOUR

Grady wanted it now. Right this second. Standing above her, he absorbed her flushed cheeks and her palm flat against her chest. The view was breathtaking, and he wanted to touch, taste, hear, see, feel. He wanted the heat of Jordana's skin against him, her flavor in his mouth, her lips crushed beneath his. He wanted all that so badly it was hard to force a breath into his lungs.

He was totally out of control. He was supposed to be doing this for... what was his wife's name?

Of course he knew her name. But that was the Jordana effect, making him *want* to forget everything else. Her words had seduced him even from the small screen of his phone. This was crazy. Last week, she'd been just another admin sitting outside the executive offices.

He should get the hell out right now. Run.

Instead, he rolled Ivy's chair into Jordana's cubicle. He could have asked her why that incident had been her most erotic, but his body understood instinctively. It was the unexpectedness of it, accompanied by a desire that had most certainly been simmering between her and the colleague for a week. He needed to know more. "Tell me the second most erotic thing you've ever done."

"But this is *your* lesson," she emphasized. "I'm not supposed to do all the talking."

Deep breath in, out, he focused on keeping his voice steady. "Isn't the point of the lesson about inducing—" He hesitated, searching for the right word, not finding it. "—a certain reaction?"

She laughed, fanned her prettily flushed cheeks. "Well, someone's certainly having a reaction."

She didn't know the half of it. She'd seduced herself with her memories, but she'd completely rolled him under, swirled him around, and tossed him up on a deserted island where only the next words out of her mouth could satisfy his hunger.

"So tell me," he said softly, his gaze on her plump lips and the swell of her breasts in his peripheral vision as she breathed deeply. He imagined he could smell her rising heat, her aroused body.

Each beat of his heart was a separate staccato burst as he waited for her answer. She tucked her chestnut hair behind her ear, then smiled the most singularly seductive smile he'd ever seen. If his pulse had been even close to normal, that smile would have jammed it into instant overdrive.

"The summer before I graduated from college, I worked in a really small office for a machine shop." Her lips puckered around the last sound. "All those big, burly men working with their hands." She shivered dramatically.

Her voice seeped into his blood. He couldn't even prompt her with a word, just a soft grunt.

"The foreman was constantly in and out of my office with one thing or another. He was as attracted to me as I was to him."

Who wouldn't be? His mouth went dry with his attraction, despite how wrong it was.

"One day he was helping me with a purchase order." Her voice dropped. "Hunkered down next to my chair, his legs bracketed my knees on either side, holding me in place." She demonstrated with her hands, waving them around her knees, as if that would help Grady see the man hemming her in.

"He was so close, I could feel the heat of his skin. I swear I heard his heart beating faster and saw the rushing pulse at his neck." She closed her eyes longer than a blink, as if she could see it all again, even feel it. "And I could smell him. Not sweaty, but salty and male."

"Like a locker room?" He made the joke to ease his own inner tension.

She pressed her lips together in a don't-get-me-started smile. "*Not* like a locker room. It was totally sexual. The way a man smells, just his skin, not cologne, not aftershave, but…" She shrugged with that sexy shimmy of hers, lifting her eyebrows, too. "Big, hot male."

He knew what she meant. It was like trying to describe the scent of woman, all the lotions she used mixing with her own unique scent. Jordana's scent was like an orange grove, slightly sweet but tart as well, clean and fresh.

"Is that what you find attractive about a man, the way he smells?"

A teasing light sparkled in her eyes, along with the smallest of smiles. "His scent, his looks, his body," she agreed. "But he has to be able to make me laugh. And I don't like a mean streak." She leaned forward in her chair, the curve of her breast visible against her tight shirt. "It's actually hard to define. I was very attracted to a boss of mine who was quite large. There was something about the deepness of his voice, as if I could feel it inside me." She put her hand to her chest, driving the heat factor up yet again. "Every man is different. Some can be drop-dead gorgeous, but they leave me drop-dead cold."

Grady didn't ask how he rated. "So your foreman smelled good. Did he touch you?"

"Not then." She twirled her fingers in her pink beaded necklace. "He looked. I looked. Then one morning I had to come in early to talk to a supplier back east. The shop was empty. Except for him." A pulse began to race at her throat. "He told me he'd been daydreaming about me on the drive home from work."

"That was bold."

"I liked it. Women like bold. If you want me, tell me. Don't pussyfoot."

Another lesson. He was bold in business, but since he'd been with Darlene for so long, he'd lost his boldness with women. Yeah, he'd been totally complacent. *Sweetheart, I want to do this filthy dirty thing to you that you're going to absolutely love, and I want it right freaking now.* That was bold. He'd never tried it. Never even thought of it. Wasn't even sure what filthy, dirty, sexy, hot thing he wanted.

Until Jordana told him.

"He said he'd been dreaming about putting his mouth on me, making me come that way. For hours. Until I couldn't stand it anymore."

Grady's breath rushed out of him, leaving his lungs

starving, his brain foggy, and his body hard.

"So he did," she whispered. There was just her voice, deep inside him, the way she'd described feeling her boss's voice. "Right there in the stockroom. He set me on a stool, lifted my skirt." She paused, letting him feel the slide of material up her thighs. "I've never wanted to scream so badly in my life, but we had to be silent in case someone came in early."

He could hear his harsh breathing in the wake of her words, but he was incapable of ratchetting it down.

"Do you understand why it was so good?" she asked softly, gently prying at his thoughts.

He understood on a cellular level, in his bones, his heart. "He'd been thinking about you for days, weeks. And he was beyond his limit. He had to have you."

"Oh, Mr. Masterson, you're such a good pupil."

He was. Too good. Because he felt the same thing. Maybe he had voyeuristic tendencies, getting off on stories, fantasies, words. On her voice.

He swallowed hard, his throat clicking with the effort. "I'm just not sure how to use the technique on my wife." The observation was like a cold dousing, over his head and down the back of his dress shirt. He'd needed the drenching. Jordana was getting to him. A bucket of cold water between them was exactly what he required, unless he wanted to throw her to the carpet right now, lift her crazily sexy skirt, and taste her for hours.

"It's the element of surprise." Her voice was completely neutral now, as if she were talking to Rhonda. "And trying something new. Liiike…" She lingered over the word, thinking, then suddenly rushed on. "You're painting the living room and she's down on all floors taping the baseboards, wearing teeny-tiny shorts because it's a hot day."

Darlene didn't wear teeny-tiny shorts. She was always elegant and well-groomed. And they would never paint the living room together. They'd hire someone to do it, but he didn't need to tell Jordana that, not when she was on a roll.

"Suddenly you can't resist pulling down those shorts." She wrinkled her nose and raised an eyebrow. "And doing what men do." She fluttered her eyelashes. "See what I mean?"

He saw. Her imagination amazed him. Or was that a real scenario?

He scratched a divot in the plastic arm of the chair. "So did you start dating your foreman?"

She had such a sweetly sly smile, secretive and knowing. "I don't date. I'm a career girl."

Jordana was as unique as they came. She didn't date, she didn't stay overnight with a man, and she loved sex. "But don't you want to get married and have children?" These days, a woman could handle both, career and family. And he wanted to know more about her.

"Sure I want to have kids someday." She gave a little toss of her hair. "But he has to be the right man. Someone steady, who's going to be there. I don't want some deadbeat dad who'll suddenly decide he doesn't want to be a father anymore."

Interesting that her requirement wasn't about sex or desire but only about a good father for her future children. "The foreman wasn't the right man?"

"No. I know the difference between lust and love. You can lust after a bad boy, but you fall for a steady guy." She crossed her legs and settled back in her chair. "The closest I ever came was with a friend I'd known for years. We never dated, and we never had sex. But I could have loved him, I think."

"What happened?"

"He got married."

Grady watched her closely. She didn't seem sad about unrequited love, merely wistful.

"Anyway, I'm not in a rush," she went on. "And I'm not settling for Mr. Deadbeat Dad just so I can have kids, especially when my career is more important right now." She shot him the sly smile again. "In the meantime, I don't think I should have to miss out on lust. Do you?"

"No."

"But you probably think I'm some sort of female Casanova. Seducing men, leaving them." She waved a hand breezily.

"I like the way you think. Sex should be fun."

"Right," she said brightly. "Without all the angst and anger and hurt that make everything dreary."

Her attitude about love, marriage, and sex was completely refreshing. There was a difference of more than ten years between them, but he was still of a generation that believed women ultimately wanted to be mothers and wives and that sex for them was better if it involved love.

Jordana dispelled all the myths.

Then it hit him that Darlene did, too. She'd made it very clear she didn't want children, that their careers were more important. And they'd been happy.

Except that *they* hadn't been. Only he had.

"You're thinking." Jordana was suddenly there in the room with him again.

For long moments, he felt like he'd disappeared. "Just a quick thought."

"You were getting angry." She looked at him, *into* him.

He could feel her eyes on the inside of his brain. "You're too intuitive."

"I'm in HR. We have to be. It's a very psychological job, trying to figure out what people want." She planted her elbows on her desk, laced her fingers and rested her chin on top. "And you were getting angry about your wife."

"Yeah," he admitted.

"Lesson number whatever: Don't get angry."

"Get even," he finished for her.

She clucked her tongue like an old maid. "No. Get better at whatever she needs."

"Miss Oh-so-wise, that's my problem. I don't know what she needs."

"Then ask her."

He scoffed. "Is anything that simple?"

"Of course not. But you've got to start somewhere." She shoved back from the desk and rolled her chair to the other side. Opening a file drawer, she dug inside, then tossed a granola bar at him. He caught it.

"All that sexy talk made me starving." She peeled the wrapper like a banana.

He was starving, too. Not for food, but for the things she'd awakened in him.

God, that was close. Jordana had almost seduced herself. She'd told her hot little story, imagining Grady in her foreman's starring role.

If he hadn't gone into some inner place, she might actually have tried to draw him in again, tell him another story. Or make something up. But he'd started thinking about his wife, clearly indicated by the deep line drawing his eyebrows together, and that reminded her *everything* was about his wife.

"So call her tonight," she told him.

Grady was slouched in his chair, chewing the last bite of the granola bar. "Phone sex isn't going to work at this point."

God, he made her laugh. Even when he wasn't trying to. That could be a problem. She was a sucker for a man with a sense of humor. "Not phone sex. Or email sex. All that stuff is for when you're talking to each other again. When you've needled a chink into her armor. For now, you should just…" What should he do? What would she, as a woman, want him to do? Not that she was anything like his wife, but sometimes a woman could intuit these things better than a man.

Grady steepled his fingers, waiting solemnly for her next brilliant remark.

She closed her eyes. Looking at his handsome face distracted her. His wife said he was too vanilla, which translated to her needing to feel desired. Which meant Grady had to be wild and crazy. But he couldn't just call her up and start spouting sexy, dirty words. First he had to…

She opened her eyes and found his dark, too sexy gaze pouring over her. "You have to tell her you'll do anything to win her back. Ask what she really wants. Really, truly."

He looked at her for the count of three, then stuck his hand in his pocket. He came out with his phone. "Shall I do it now and you can coach me?"

She groaned. "Noo." Her lips rounded on the long sound. "Tonight. When you're in bed. When she's in bed and ready to fall asleep."

"That might work on you, but it's not going to work on her."

Would it work on Jordana? She didn't do relationships. Before leaving her last job, she'd started seeing one of the accountants, and though occasionally they'd gone to a movie or out for dinner or drinks, mostly it was sex. He'd ended it six months ago because he met a girl he wanted to date. Jordana had been totally fine with it, though she missed the sex.

Her only real relationship had been with her best friend, Eddie, down in L.A. Her mom had been a bartender. She still lived and worked down there, though Jordana rarely saw her. Her mom had been totally ready for her to get out of the house. As a teen, Jordana was alone a lot, and Eddie kept her company. They'd gone to middle school and high school together, then junior college. Until she left L.A. for San Francisco. They'd never been about sex or love. Angsty emotions hadn't tainted their friendship. She'd loved him for who he was, for being her steady rock, and probably also because she didn't have to live with the things that would have ticked her off. She might have fallen *in* love with him eventually, when they were both ready—when *she* was ready—but for sure they would still be friends if he hadn't met a girl while Jordana was in San Francisco. His new wife hadn't been comfortable with Eddie having a female best friend. A dead giveaway was her refusal to allow Jordana to be a member of the wedding party, not as a bridesmaid but as Eddie's best man, or, well, his best woman. She still missed Eddie. She missed knowing his two little kids. Maybe she was even angry that he hadn't stood up for her, refused to give up his best friend, left her without a call or a birthday card. Just like her dad. Eddie was the reason—not the weather and less smog as she'd claimed—that she'd decided to stay in the Bay Area instead of going back to L.A after college.

And that all said she *didn't* know what Grady's wife wanted. She didn't know what women who enjoyed relationships really wanted. Being a self-proclaimed desire junkie, Jordana knew only about desire. "Just apologize then. You were angry the night you got the email. Tell her you regret some of the stuff you said."

He studied her a moment. "What makes you think I haven't already called her?"

She eyed him right back. "Have you?"

His eyes slid to the left, a definite nonverbal cue.

"Didn't think so," she said. "It's been a week. Don't say you're waiting for her to call first."

"Actually I was too busy watching chick flicks."

She laughed. "Liar. I had to force you to watch the first one." She really did enjoy his wit. "You don't want to call her?"

She counted his breaths, five of them, before he said, "I'm not ready not to yell at her."

"It's good that you don't want to yell."

Three more breaths. "I need to learn more about how

women think before I approach her."

"I'm trying to help with that."

"And you're helping a lot."

But should she? His gaze was so intense it was slightly unnerving. The things she'd tried teaching him so far had only made her think of him as a man. A very attractive man. *Not* a married man, with a wife who'd dumped him over email. Without a doubt, she *was* flirting with him. And enjoying it. But maybe she was going too far.

"Okay," she told him, "tonight watch *Buffy the Vampire Slayer.*" Which had nothing to do with teaching him how to talk to his wife. That was about kissing. And wild, crazy sex.

She rolled to the file drawer containing her granola bars and purse. "That's enough teaching material for tonight."

"Last night I studied James's method of kissing."

Her body started to hum. "That's good. Very good." She stood, but her legs felt slightly wobbly, as if she'd just had really good sex.

He remained seated. "I understand how it works."

His eyes on her topped out her thermometer. "All it takes is practice."

God, she wanted him to practice on her. She hadn't been with anyone in six months. That was way too long, and it made her edgy. It made her ripe for a little work dalliance, more than just a flirtation. Bad idea, *very* bad, especially if she dallied with Grady. She edged around his chair, backing away. She should have reminded him to call his wife, but she couldn't get the words out. "I'll come up with another lesson for tomorrow."

He swiveled slightly, watching her. "Yes. Do that."

"And make sure you delete all our texts off your phone." She was pretty far gone with desire, but not too far gone to forget the reminder. And to remind herself. No matter how hot he made her, she could never forget how important her job was. The desire junkie in her ignored the little voice inside saying—no, shouting—that she shouldn't be doing any of this at all. The problem was that she'd always been a risk-taker when it came to desire.

"Good idea," Grady said, his eyes saying he meant something else entirely.

It was time to go. *Now.* "See ya." She made her mouth stretch into a smile.

He stretched one back at her.

Then she turned the corner, and damn if she didn't almost run, afraid he'd be after her like James went after Jane Austen and Penelope.

If Grady made a move on her, she'd let him do anything.

CHAPTER FIVE

Grady held onto the arms of the chair until his fingers turned white and his knuckles ached. He literally held himself down waiting for the outer door beyond the warren of cubicles to close behind her.

He'd wanted to lunge at Jordana. Take her mouth. Taste her. Kiss her senseless. Until *he* was senseless.

"It's lust," he whispered to the empty building. "Nothing good can happen."

He eased his grip on the chair. His phone lay on the desk, its silence shouting at him.

Darlene hadn't called him. He hadn't called her. He hadn't received any divorce papers from her attorney nor had he contacted a lawyer himself. He was still married.

What he felt about Jordana was craziness.

He put his hand on his cell, his fingers slowly curling around it. Picking it up, he held it a long moment. Then he keyed in his pass code. The bright background leapt out. He read the outside temperature and the time. He reread the chain of sexts. Then deleted them. Though he would have preferred to keep the string, trashing them was safer for Jordana. And for him. Finally he tapped his contacts list, bringing up the favorites. Darlene's face smiled from her icon. He punched her nose. Then he pushed the speaker button because he felt too lazy to hold the phone to his ear.

He hadn't needed Jordana to tell him he should talk to his wife. He knew it, but he'd been avoiding it. He didn't want to deal with Darlene. Or think about what he was doing. Or would be doing. Divorce, selling the house, moving, rearranging his life. Or begging her to come back so that nothing had to change. Fixing a marriage was a daunting task. Maybe that's why everyone got divorced. It was so much easier than repairing what had gone wrong. Just trying to figure out where you'd both deviated from the plan was nightmarish. He envisioned couple's counseling, baring his heart and soul, then having to change the things about himself that he was comfortable with even if she wasn't.

Darlene's voicemail kicked in before she answered. Her cell phone was an extension of her hand, so if she didn't take his call, it was because she didn't want to. Or she was in the bathroom. Although, he'd known her to take the phone with her even in there.

He didn't leave a message. If she really, truly hadn't been able to answer the phone—doubtful—she'd get the missed-call alert.

His chair was still swiveled toward the door through which Jordana had beat her hasty retreat. That had been good for both of them. If she'd remained, he might very well have taken a dive at her.

She intrigued him beyond comprehension. Her

openness about sex and relationships was intoxicating. She just wanted to have sex. That was all. She didn't need all the trappings. She was a woman a man could feel free to lust after without any complications or requirements. No thought, no mess, no guilt. Except about Darlene. But Darlene had left him with nothing more than an email after their twenty-year relationship, fifteen of marriage and five of dating. Almost half their lives.

What the hell was he feeling?

He wasn't raging. He wasn't broken. He wasn't even lonely.

Instead he was obsessed with a woman twelve years younger than himself.

It all boiled down to the one question he hadn't asked himself yet. Did he still love Darlene enough to fight for her?

His lack of loyalty, stamina, and integrity was galling to him. And yet…

He looked at the phone in his hand. Darlene hadn't called. She didn't want to come back. She was having a midlife crisis. Maybe she had a lover despite her denials. He didn't know for sure. Maybe he was just an unfeeling bastard, and that's why she left him.

When was the last time he'd felt strong emotion about anything? He couldn't remember. He wondered if he ever had. He and Darlene hadn't fought. Everything had been… stable. Complacent. He was always steady, never particularly demonstrative. Sex was good, but not wild. Even in the beginning, he hadn't constantly thought about Darlene, as if he couldn't get enough of her. He'd had his classes, grades to maintain, the rowing team he was on, a large family with all the gatherings at which attendance was expected. There were other things in his life besides Darlene. He'd never been wild, crazy, infatuated to the point he couldn't think of anything else. There could be something wrong with him. Maybe he was coldblooded.

But he was sure as hell turned hot-blooded around Jordana Davis. She made every nerve light up, every cell tremble. He couldn't remember ever feeling like this before.

Maybe Darlene wasn't the only one having a midlife crisis.

Since their tête-à-tête a week ago—when Jordana had told him all her erotic stories and almost begged him to try out his newly acquired kissing technique on her—Grady was getting the hang of sexting. Boy, was he ever getting the hang. He'd pried out more of Jordana's tales, and by the end of some of their little sessions—which they did outside of strict work hours for the most part—Jordana was dying. She needed a man. Her trusty device just wasn't enough after going at it verbally—albeit silently—with Grady. Sexting was supposed to be a prelude to things that would happen later, but without being able to act on it, all those sexy texts just might be the death of her. Literally. How much more could she take?

But Grady loved her stories. He wasn't the judgmental sort of man who thought a woman's desire to have casual sex was synonymous with crass. Or that casual sex itself was crass. She believed that sex was meant to be enjoyed. Love wasn't one of its limits. And Grady seemed to appreciate that about her.

As far as she knew, he hadn't talked to his wife. She hadn't asked him, and he hadn't offered the information. But it was two weeks now since the woman had email-divorced him. They really needed to talk. Not Jordana's business, though.

It was late Thursday afternoon. Between interruptions from Rhonda, plus moving to the conference room to host a parade of employees with questions—she should have her own office if she was going to constantly discuss sensitive issues—she worked on Rhonda's latest brainstorm, compiling a list of employee emergency contact numbers that managers could use in, yes, an emergency. Except that it was easier to simply look an employee up on the system in the event of an emergency. But gosh, Rhonda thought—she really shouldn't think so much—what if there was an earthquake? You couldn't look up *all* those employees.

If there was an earthquake, they'd have bigger things to worry about.

It was busy work. Rhonda liked busy-work projects, even if they were really just a matter of writing a query to pull out the data. Of course, in the process, Jordana figured out they didn't have everyone's emergency contact information. That was the real project that needed attention. Maybe she could borrow Ivy to help with that when there was a lull in activity. Grady often lent her Ivy's assistance. He was great that way. And in other ways…

Suddenly something dropped right in her lap, bouncing a little on her tight skirt. A crumpled piece of paper. She stared at it a moment, looked up. No one there, not even a shadow. She glanced sideways into Rhonda's office. Her boss was on the phone, her lips pinched in mid-argument.

Jordana smoothed out the paper and read: *I need more advice. Meet me at Leo's at five-thirty? My treat.*

At least he'd added a question mark so it didn't look like a command from God or the CEO. And he'd offered to pay.

Leo's was a yuppie bar along Main Street in Menlo Park, a couple of miles from the office. It was possible they might be seen by someone from work, though it was a Thursday evening rather than Friday, which lessened the likelihood of being spotted. Although, if they were seen, no one would be too suspicious. After all, if they *were* sneaking around, they would hardly sneak into Leo's. It was almost like hiding in plain sight. She didn't want to become someone else's gossip, and Grady didn't deserve it. Leo's was safe in other ways, too. They wouldn't be alone together. She couldn't beg him to test out his kissing techniques. This wasn't escalation because he only wanted another lesson. And the bar had fabulous Happy Hour appetizers. It was a win-win. Or rationalization.

She texted a quick *okay* to him. Why did he throw a note in her lap instead of texting? But it had been kind of sexy.

She shut her computer down a little after five, grabbed her purse, waved at Rhonda, ignored Grady's open door, and headed to the ladies' room to freshen up.

Two miles in Silicon Valley freeway traffic during rush hour could take half an hour. She made it through surface streets with five minutes to spare, but had to circle like a buzzard searching for road kill until she found a parking spot. Menlo Park was a trendy dinner spot, and she didn't want to miss Happy Hour.

Grady already had a table. The tops were miniscule, room for a pitcher of beer, a few glasses, and two small plates of appetizers. If you were lucky, you could squish five chairs around the table, but you had to stretch for your glass and food. Grady had guarded a seat for her, but amid all the other chairs and people around them, her knee was crammed against his when she sat down, his heat washing over her bare legs.

He leaned closer, speaking over the noise, his breath against her ear warm and pleasantly yeasty with beer. "I ordered a champagne cocktail for you."

She glanced at the fizzing liquid, tinged with pink. "How did you know?"

He shrugged. "The last Christmas party. I wondered what it was. My wife told me."

She felt an odd mixture of hot and cold. She'd been a new hire then, yet he'd noticed her while he'd been with his wife. Of course, that probably meant there'd been nothing to it. Still, she liked it. Too much.

"Thank you." She craned to look at the Happy Hour buffet. "I'm hungry."

He rose before she could. "I'll get you something."

While he was gone, she scanned the crowd for familiar faces and saw none. All the seats were taken along the mahogany bar, a second layer of people standing. With the warm weather, the front doors were open onto the outside patio. Everywhere, people and chairs were crammed in like mackerel squished in a can. The waitresses waded through with trays held high, a wave of buffet goers following in their wake trying to get back to their tables.

Paying for the food was handled at the end of the buffet line. There were no seconds, and you piled whatever you could onto your plate. But it was cheap and good.

Grady returned with fried artichoke hearts, carrot sticks, and mini quiches. "All the major food groups," he said.

She scarfed an artichoke heart, a quiche that disappeared in one bite, and two carrot sticks. She finished it all with a low growl in her throat. "God, I was hungry."

Grady stared at her.

"Thank you?" It ended on a question. Because there was something expectant in his gaze. Or speculative? She wasn't sure. His eyes were dark, his pupils wide, his look somehow… potent.

"Do you always make that sound when you eat?"

"What sound?"

"That purr. Like a cat who's just been satisfied extremely well."

Her pulse throbbed right down into her fingertips. "I always make that sound when I'm satisfied."

If possible, his eyes got darker. They both knew she wasn't talking about food. She sipped her champagne and purred for him again. "I needed that, too."

There was a burst of raucous laughter, but she thought she heard him ask, "What other satisfaction do you need?"

She leaned closer, an excuse to inhale his male scent. "I'm sorry, I didn't quite catch that."

He waited only a beat before saying, "I'm glad you enjoyed it."

Chicken. Then again, she could have assumed she'd heard correctly and told him exactly what kind of satisfaction she needed. Who was the chicken now? She imagined what was going through his mind, the wild things he might want to do to her. She knew it was crazy, but the sexting had taken her over, made her feel out of control. Maybe that was why she'd agreed to meet him so easily, because she could no longer help herself. Desire was actually taking her over.

His eyes on her, he raised his beer and took two swallows before setting it back down. "You said I should call my wife. I did. She didn't answer."

She quelled the urge to laugh. *No, Jordana, everything isn't about you.* Of course, he'd been thinking about his wife. "Does that bother you?"

"I'm bothered." He waited a moment, going on when she didn't make a comment. "Which is why I wanted your advice." He grimaced. "Not advice, per se, just more answers."

Her heart took a tiny plunge. He wasn't asking for more of her stories. "About what?"

"Women want to be desired. They want their men crazy for them. Wild. Insane." He spoke without even looking around to check if they were overheard, and his eyes were hot with seriousness. "I get that. But what happens after the sex? What do you want then?"

She toyed with the stem of her champagne flute, turning it on the table. "It depends on the man and the level of my attraction."

"The foreman," he said quickly. "You didn't want to date him."

She remembered their sexy sessions. "I liked the riskiness of it. Coming in early. Or sneaking out at lunch. Or driving to a secluded spot after hours."

"But what did you want from him afterward? Did you want him to call you at night? Did you want him to keep upping the desire quotient?" He leaned closer, intense, as if everything important hung on her answer.

She wet her lips, his eyes tracking the glide of her tongue. "He called me late at night sometimes. I liked that. I liked all the secret looks between us. The stolen touches when he'd run his hand down my thigh."

"So you wanted him constantly thinking about you. You wanted him to demonstrate how he felt."

"Well, yeah, I guess. But not to the point where he cut off his finger while using the lathe."

He sat back, a smile ghosting over his lips. "Sort of like Vincent van Gogh cutting off his ear for love of a woman?"

"I don't think he did that because of a woman. I think he was pissed off at Gauguin."

"I wouldn't get *that* crazy. But how crazy do you want? Calling you ten times a day? Showing up at your door?"

She threw her fingers up in a cross. "Oh please, no stalker stuff. A woman just wants to have fun. Make her feel desirable." She let her lips curve slyly. "Then be on your way." She fluttered her hand as if shooing away an annoying bug.

"Until the next time you need me."

"Exactly."

He held his hand over his beer mug on the table, regarding her for long moments. "How long did it last with the foreman?"

"I'm not sure. A month and a half maybe."

"Why did you stop?"

She lifted one shoulder in a half shrug. "Summer ended and I went back to college."

"But you could have seen him after that."

His questions made her take a deep breath. She hadn't spent summers at home in L.A. Eddie had already left her for the other woman so she'd stayed in the Bay Area and taken summer jobs. She could have seen the foreman again. "That would be more like dating. And it was my senior year with a lot of heavy classes. I didn't have time for dating."

"But—"

She held up a hand, stopping him. Her heart was beating too fast, and not in a good way. "Look, if you're trying to psychoanalyze me and figure out why I like short-term, casual relationships—"

"I'm not psychoanalyzing *you*." He propped his elbows on the table and laced his fingers, his knee bumping up against hers with an electric jolt. "I told you I like the way you think. It's uncomplicated. More people should be like that."

"So you don't think I'm slutty."

He laughed, one loud bark that turned heads their way. His eyes were shining. "Definitely not. That's a negative term. Yurrrrr…" He kept the word going until he found the one he wanted. "A temptress."

This time she laughed, sexy but softer than him so that eyes didn't swivel toward them. "Very old-fashioned."

"But appropriate. Your attitude tempts men. With all your subtle ways, you let them know what you want. They're intrigued because they've never met anyone like you, a woman who doesn't have a bunch of expectations she's dying to lay on them. You're irresistible."

Her hands were warm. Her thighs were hot. Every centimeter of her body heated for him. "That's what women want," she whispered. "To make you feel like that. To be irresistible to you."

He dropped his eyes, swallowed two big gulps of his beer, and came up coughing. She pounded his back until he wiped his eyes, gasping, "Sorry."

"You really do know how to make a woman feel irresistible," she told him.

His jaw worked a moment, as if he was grinding his teeth. "I don't know how to make my wife feel that way."

She didn't shudder. She hadn't forgotten this was all about his wife. She wouldn't deny that she liked the sexual tension simmering between them. It was fun, sexy, all the things she looked for. But she couldn't forget his wife. "It's a lot harder when you know someone, and there's all sorts of baggage you have to get through first."

"Is that why you didn't marry your best friend?"

She thumped back in her chair. "What do you mean?"

"You knew everything about him. He couldn't excite you anymore." He had a very steady, penetrating gaze, and he saw too much with it.

Part of excitement was in not knowing what to expect, in hearing things for the first time, in not being able to read a man's mind. Sure you sensed the attraction, but you didn't know exactly what he was thinking. With Eddie, there weren't any surprises. He was kind, sweet, and always treated her exactly the same. She predicted what he was going to say before he said it, guessed what choice he would make in any decision. She knew everything about him. It had been so comfortable, like a favorite jacket you needed when the weather suddenly turned stormy. She had friends, but she missed having a friend like Eddie, the person she could say anything to. But…

"I'm not sure he ever excited me that way." Maybe she'd never really given him a chance to. What if she'd let things go a little further? What if she'd let Eddie surprise her? He might not have abandoned her. But she didn't want to talk about Eddie so she turned the conversation back on Grady. "When did your wife stop exciting you?"

"She didn't."

She gave him the same level gaze he'd given her, without saying a word.

He caved. "Obviously I'm the one who doesn't excite her."

With a burst of laughter from the next table, she had to lean closer once more. "Honestly? Are you really telling me that you raced home from work every night dying to drag her into the bedroom?" She widened her eyes at him. "Or better yet, you couldn't even wait to get her into the bedroom. You had to have her right there in the kitchen while she was making dinner. You just flipped up her little flowered apron, and—"

"Darlene doesn't wear flowered aprons and she doesn't make dinner." His features were completely deadpan.

She gave a prim little sniff. "And the fact that she doesn't cook bugs you?"

"That would make her too much like my mother." His voice was taut, with an equal stiffness in his shoulders. "Not that I don't love my mother. I just don't want to be married to her."

Jordana put her hand over her mouth and laughed into her palm. "You're too funny." She plopped her fisted hands on her hips. "Okay, what I'm talking about is the surprise. You have to figure out how to amaze her." Maybe he needed to surprise himself. "When's the last time you took her on a spur-of-the-moment adventure?"

He blinked, as if he couldn't figure out how she'd gotten from his wife not wearing an apron to an exciting adventure. But he had an answer. "We went up to Napa for a day in May."

"Whose plan was that?" she tossed back at him.

He looked to the left side of the room, then the right, and finally at back at Jordana. "Hers."

She chided him with a shake of her finger. "See, that's the thing men don't get. We want *you* to plan the trip. Book the cute little bed-and-breakfast. Decide all the fun things we're going to do. Choose the restaurants. Take care of everything." She hadn't taken any trips with a man, but if she was going to, that's what she'd want.

Taking his beer in hand again, twirling it in the ring of condensation on the table, he said, "So, I'm supposed to come home and drag her into the bedroom to have my wicked way with her. Then I tell her about the trip I've planned forrrr…" He trailed the word out, just like he had before, until he had a thought to toss at her. "A weekend stay in Maui at the Westin."

She clapped her hands to both his cheeks. "Oh my God. Whisk her away for a sexy weekend in the sun. You're absolutely brilliant."

He was close enough for her to see the green flecks in his forest-dark eyes. His lips were so close, his male scent a tease. She felt herself falling, wanting to taste him. Wanting the Maui trip. Wanting *him*.

CHAPTER SIX

The music and the voices and the laughter were pounding in his head, beating out a jungle rhythm that commanded him to grab Jordana, crush his mouth to hers, and kiss her until he couldn't remember who he was. Until he didn't *want* to remember. He wanted to haul her away to his bedroom and have his wicked way with her. He imagined her in a little flowered apron and nothing else.

Coming here had been a bad idea, but all the texts over the last week had scrambled his brain cells, and he'd just wanted to sit and talk. To look at her. And drink in her scent. Oh yeah, he'd lost his mind.

Grady spread his fingers flat on the table. It was the only way to keep his hands off her. Because she wanted this as much as he did. Her gaze shouted it, her soft lips begged for it. He'd thought a busy, noisy, teeming bar would stifle all the sexual tension surrounding them like a fog. But it was worse. He had to sit closer to hear her, lean in to make out her words. Every time someone moved at the table next to him, his thigh was shoved into hers. Her tangy citrus scent beguiled him. He wanted to know everything about her, the foreman, the best friend who'd married someone else, the man who hadn't planned a vacation for her, the one who'd put her hand between his legs. He wanted to know every erotic thing she'd ever done and why it aroused her.

The only thing that broke the spell was his wife's name. He invoked it now before he did something he couldn't take back. "So I should just show up at Darlene's hotel room."

Jordana pulled back, her hands falling away, her eyes dropping. "Yes." She sipped her champagne, and he couldn't tear his gaze away from her mouth as she licked a drop from her lower lip. "Do you know where she's staying?"

He shook his head, something inside him twisting at the sudden distance between them. He wanted her hands on him again. But as angry as he was at Darlene, he wasn't a quitter. And he couldn't exact revenge by taking what he wanted from Jordana. It wouldn't be fair to her. "I don't know. She's not answering her cell. But she'll answer at work tomorrow." She wouldn't know it was him if he used her direct line. He could have called the number already, but he hadn't. He was stewing. He was falling into Jordana.

"Good idea." She finished the champagne, a long swallow that starting him sweating all over again as the column of her throat mesmerized him. "I better go," she said, pushing the glass away.

"What's my next lesson?" He didn't want her to leave, even though he knew she should. He stopped short of grabbing her arm to hold her down. That's when things had gone crazy earlier, when she'd put her hands on his face. Touching was bad. Touching was a step too far over the line. Touching made him want things he couldn't have.

"At this point you need to talk to her. None of my lessons will work if you don't even know where she is." She slung the strap of her purse over her head, where it slipped down between her breasts, outlining them against her shirt. He saw the vaguest shape of her nipple.

"Right. Talk to her." He dragged his eyes back to her face. And that was a bad idea, too. Because her lips were so damn kissable. And she smelled insanely good.

She stood, still close in the confined space around the tables. He should have risen, too, so her breasts weren't at eye level, but there wasn't an inch of room to push his chair back. At least that was his excuse.

"Tell me good news tomorrow," she said. "And thanks for the drink and the appetizers."

He let her go this time. There was no other choice. He was married. She was teaching him how to get his wife back. Anything else was just a fantasy he didn't have any right to contemplate.

Grady needed to call Darlene. It was no good letting things sit unresolved between them. If she was having an affair, he'd deal with it, but their marriage deserved a face-to-face.

Out in Leo's parking lot, the six-thirty sun was still bright. Somehow he'd felt as if he'd been with Jordana for hours. That was a clear indication that he needed to stop thinking about her.

He called Darlene's cell first, and when she didn't answer, he called her office. She didn't answer there either. She worked at an investment house on University Ave in Palo Alto, not that far from Leo's in Menlo Park. He took El Camino to get there, and the traffic was heavy. University Ave was jam-packed for the dinner hour, with nary a parking space available, and the crowds at the bars and restaurants spilling out onto the sidewalks. It didn't matter whether it was a weekend or a weeknight, the quaint main street of Palo Alto was always busy. Good for him that Darlene's office building had a private lot. The attendant at the gate knew him and let him in. The spaces were half full, and he found Darlene's car toward the back in the shade of a big oak, an empty spot next to it. It was possible she was in a meeting or with a client, and that's why she hadn't answered her office phone. Not wanting to force a confrontation in front of her colleagues, he didn't go inside. Instead, he leaned on the trunk of her car and waited. Fifteen minutes later, she exited the building.

And she wasn't alone.

His wife was gorgeous. At forty-two, she had the body and face of a woman ten years younger. Her skirts had gotten shorter over the last couple of years, as if turning forty had made her want to show off her fabulous legs while she still could. Her thick, glossy brunette hair shone with red highlights in the sun, swinging across her shoulders as she swayed sexily in her spiked heels.

She didn't see him leaning against her car. She only had eyes for the man walking beside her. She laughed at something he said. The man smiled. They weren't aware of a single thing in that parking lot except each other. Darlene didn't touch him, and he didn't touch her, but there was an intimacy in their closeness, their heads bent together, the smiles, the laughter, the way her hip occasionally bumped his as they walked.

Grady's collar grew too hot around his neck. His jaw ached until he realized he was clenching his teeth. A blaze burned inside his chest, and his hands were balled into fists. Even in the shade of the oak, it was suddenly brutally hot, and he wanted to tear off his suit jacket, throw it down on the shimmering concrete like a gauntlet they would have to cross over.

His gut had known she was cheating, yet there'd been a massive part of him that wanted to be wrong. But seeing her with Mr. GQ—his suit expensive and tailored, his hair a perfect blond contrast to her brunette—Grady felt the blood coagulate in his heart.

Leaning against the trunk, his clothes blending with the black paint job and the shade tree, she didn't see him until she lifted her hand to fire her remote at the car. She jumped away from Mr. GQ so quickly she almost fell off her heels. When the man put out a hand to her, she jerked away.

Guilt had made her falter. If it was nothing, she wouldn't act like a trapped woman.

But Darlene couldn't be kept down for long. She righted herself, laughed at her clumsiness, and walked to the car with several paces between her and her lover.

"Darlene," Grady said. "I was hoping I'd catch you here since I haven't been able to reach you over the phone." And she'd been caught, all right.

"I've been busy, Grady."

He glanced over her shoulder at Mr. GQ. Oh yeah, she'd been busy. Grady wanted to swat the smug look off the guy's handsome face. He was younger, maybe thirty-five, and Grady had never seen him at any of the company functions he'd attended with Darlene.

"Despite how busy you've been—" He grimaced a smile at her, and at Mr. GQ in her wake. "—we need to talk."

"It's late, Grady. Couldn't we do this another time?"

It pissed him off that she kept saying his name like he was an irritating gnat she had to bat away from her face. "No. We need to talk now."

She didn't introduce the man, but she also didn't tell him to leave. And he didn't go. He just stood a few feet away, watching, as if he thought Grady might suddenly lash out to strike Darlene.

But he'd never hit a woman and he never would.

"Grady." She couldn't leave because he was leaning on her car. She couldn't move him unless he wanted to be moved.

"Darlene."

She huffed. "All right. Let's talk."

When he looked pointedly at her lover, she turned. "Thanks so much for walking me to my car. You just can't be too careful after hours."

Grady couldn't believe she was keeping up the pretense.

Mr. GQ waited two beats, a silent, intimate look passing between them, then he said, "Sure. No problem. Have a good night." He backed up two steps, as if he still needed to keep his eye on Grady, before finally turning and striding to his Audi. Starting the engine, he gunned the motor like a warning. Or a punk teenager who wanted to make sure everyone knew he was there. Then he roared out of the parking lot.

Darlene folded her arms beneath the ample breasts she'd had enhanced seven years ago. It was an unworthy thought. But anger was simmering in him, bubbling below the surface like a quiet volcano that no one suspected was ready to blow a cloud into the air that would bury everything and everyone in its ash.

"We're not talking here," he informed her. "This deserves some time."

She shot out an irritated breath. "Grady."

Don't fucking Grady me. He didn't say it. That's how much control he still possessed. But she was pushing his limit. "After twenty years, Darlene, you can spare one hour. Since you're afraid to tell me where you're staying, let's go for a drink somewhere."

She pressed her lips together in a look so familiar he realized it was another clue he'd missed.

"I'm not afraid." She sounded haughty rather than scared, but he'd seen that tiny crack in her composure when she'd first seen him.

"Why are you fighting?" he asked. He sincerely wanted to know. "It's just a drink, just a talk. I don't get it."

She puffed out a long breath. "Fine. Let's have a drink." Then she beeped her remote again because the doors had long since relocked themselves.

Grady thought about taking her to Leo's because it would amuse him in a sick sort of way, but he wanted an intimate conversation, not one he had to shout at her.

"You can follow me over." He briefly thought she might turn in the other direction, but she had to know he'd hunt her down again.

She didn't even ask where, just climbed in her car and followed him out of the lot. He took her to a hotel on El Camino that had a quiet, intimate bar. Anywhere on University Ave would have been too noisy and too crowded. Walking side by side, they silently entered the hotel. They'd had many silent moments like this, traveling in the car for an hour, both deep in their own thoughts. This was the first time he'd ever found it uncomfortable, as if now that he had her attention, he had no idea what to say. Except to accuse.

She asked for a chardonnay. He ordered a beer. After their drinks arrived, he cut into the silence she seemed unwilling to break. "So, are you going to tell me what this really is all about?"

She pursed her lips, sucked in a breath, shot it out. "I told you in the email. We're not the same people we were fifteen years ago when we got married. I want to move on with a new phase of my life."

"With that man?" He hadn't wanted to jump right to her adultery and his cuckoldry, but she'd opened the door and he was obliged to step right through.

She flared her nostrils with irritation. "He's just a guy in the office."

"I'm not that stupid, Darlene. I saw the two of you from the moment you stepped out of the building. And he's not just a *guy in the office*," he enunciated sharply, teeth almost bared. "You're sleeping with him." He wanted to say it like it was, use all the crude and crass words for it, but that would only shut down the conversation before they'd achieved anything. If achievement was even possible at this point.

He understood her expressions and gestures like the

pages of a book he'd read every night for the last twenty years. Guilt in her dilated pupils, anger in the tight set of her mouth, frustration in her fingernail tapping against her glass, fear in the nervous bounce of her leg.

"All right fine." She shrugged, nonchalance disguising another surge of fear. "But nothing happened between us until after I left you."

He laughed. It was caustic and painful in his throat. "You were always a very good liar."

She glared at him.

"Are you afraid that if you admit the truth, I'll make sure you don't get a cent in the divorce?"

Her chin trembled, a slight telltale movement. "Is that what you want? To get nasty about this?"

His hand tightened around his beer mug, his fingers slipping in the condensation. "I want the truth. Two weeks ago, we had a marriage. Then bam, you walk out. Call me clueless, but I don't get it."

She leaned forward, her voice low and harsh. "That's the problem, you don't get it. You don't listen. You don't try to figure anything out."

"Then why didn't you just come out and tell me you weren't happy? Maybe I could have done something before you moved into a hotel and starting fucking some other guy." Shit. He had *not* meant to use that word. He hadn't meant to get angry. Well, hell, he was pissed before they started, but he hadn't meant to let it get the better of him.

"This is why I can't talk to you." She punctuated with a blazing glare. "You just start throwing around insults."

He spread his hands. "I don't know what you're talking about. We don't fight at all."

"We don't even talk, Grady." She leaned in and kept her voice low so she couldn't be overheard in the next booth, but a strident tone laced its softness. "You call and ask me what I want you to pick up for dinner. You ask me if I've had a good day. You ask me what TV show I want to watch. Then you get on your computer and do email or work or whatever. On Saturday night, you don't even ask if I want to have sex, you just assume."

He released his fingers when he realized they'd curled into fists. "Did you ever tell me you wanted something different?"

"I shouldn't have to," she said between the clench of her perfect white teeth.

"I'm not a mind reader."

"Obviously you're not." The bite in her tone took a chunk out of his hide.

He knew her signals, her expressions, her gestures, and the quieter she became, he should have asked himself why. He should have asked *her*.

But did that give her the right to walk out without a word?

"Maybe you're right." He had to give her that. "But now I'm aware. And I'm willing to go to counseling. I'm willing to learn." He didn't let himself think about his lessons with Jordana.

Darlene shook her head, that same determined set to her mouth. "It's too late. I'm in my forties now, and I want something different. I don't know what that is right now, but I can't figure it out if I'm with you."

It was like a body slam to the mat. His ears rang, his head pounded. "You want better sex?"

She tilted her chin, looked straight down her nose at

him and said, "I want someone who's engaged in sex. With me. Not just himself."

Had he really been that selfish? He couldn't stop the echo of Jordana's voice. *A woman wants to be desired. Intensely. Like you can't get enough of her. Like she's all you can think about.* He shook himself as if he could get her out of his head. "You seemed pretty satisfied with the orgasms."

Darlene's gaze was suddenly so steady, her features so perfect and still. "I was thinking about someone else."

He'd never known her to be cruel. But then he'd never known her at all. He hadn't recognized her discontent. He hadn't even thought to ask if she was satisfied. He'd just assumed she was.

"And that's your way of shutting me down," he acknowledged softly. "I have no answer for that. But I do agree with your assessment that I don't even know you anymore."

She put her teeth together, clamped her lips shut, and he could have sworn she was suddenly fighting tears. "I'm sorry it has to end like this."

"How long have you been feeling this way?" How long had she been unhappy while he was happily clueless?

She shook her head with a soft fall of her hair over the swell of her breasts. "I don't know. Years, I think."

He should shut up now. Stop asking. The truth was too brutal.

She pushed her unfinished wine away, then slid out of the booth. "I think it's time for me to go, don't you?"

He was reminded of Jordana leaving him earlier. He'd wanted to stop her. Sadly, he didn't want to stop his wife.

Nursing the beer, he sat a long time after she'd strolled through the bar, turning men's heads as she went.

She was unconsciously sexual, or maybe it was extremely conscious. She'd become a man's fantasy. It was another change he hadn't noticed.

He hadn't noticed so many things, that was true, and there was a lot of blame he could wear like a scarlet letter. But shouldn't she have told him before she wrote off their marriage without even giving him a chance, without a single word, just her nonverbal cues he'd failed completely to read?

It takes two to completely screw up a marriage. He knew his half. He hadn't understood what women wanted. He hadn't figured out how to read the signs. But he could learn. He would learn. He could figure out how to make a woman feel like she was the focus of his world, the only woman he wanted, the woman he couldn't stop thinking about. He would have to pull out all the stops, step out of his complacency, and let his inhibitions go. Instead of merely listening, he'd have to participate, say the dirty things she wanted to hear. Texting, sexting, phone sex, all of it. Every single lesson.

And he already had the perfect teacher.

CHAPTER SEVEN

Jordana slept naked. Living by herself, she didn't need sexy nighties, and rather than pajamas, she preferred a heavy comforter. She liked the weight on her. In the summer, when the comforter was way too hot, she at least wanted a sheet over her. So, that left sleeping naked whatever the season.

She wasn't quite asleep when her cell phone rang. Like usual, she'd plugged it in to charge and set it on the night table. Her heart rate jumped. It was almost eleven and since her mom, who still worked as a bartender down in L.A., wouldn't call while she was at work, all Jordana could see were bad news warning signs flashing before her eyes.

She didn't turn on the light, didn't even look at the readout, just swiped her finger across the screen to answer. "Mom?"

"Not exactly."

Her breath left her in a whoosh, and she fell back against the pillow. "You scared the crap out of me, Mr.

Masterson."

"Sorry. But after our drink this evening, I thought it was an appropriate time to call for my next lesson. Phone Sex One-oh-one." His voice was deep and sexy, maybe because it was dark or because he'd lowered it to a nighttime softness. A bedroom tone.

"I'm not sure you're ready for Phone Sex One-oh-one. We haven't finished with Sexting One-oh-one yet."

"I can take the classes concurrently. I'm sure they'll feed on each other."

He really was amusing. And he was upping the ante in their little game. "Well then, you get another gold star for taking the initiative."

"That's what a woman wants, for the man to take the initiative and assume all the risks?"

She laughed softly, and even to her own ears, it sounded seductive. "The man is *supposed* to take all the risks. If we have to initiate, we don't know for sure whether you're dying for it or you're doing it because we were handy."

"Good point. Always go for it when I want it."

"Exactly."

"Then I want another of your sexy stories."

Jordana stretched on the bed, the sheet shifting until her breasts were bared to the warm summer night and the heat in Grady's voice. There was something different about him. She couldn't quite flick the answer open with the tip of her finger, but she sensed a change. He was still asking for an erotic adventure, the way he had before, but there was an increased intensity thickening the cell waves between them.

"I've been a very bad girl over the years," she teased

his senses.

"I know. And that's what I want. Every naughty detail."

Yes, there was definitely something different. She gave him her worst, or her best, depending on one's point of view. It wasn't the most erotic, but it was certainly the riskiest. And completely exciting because of that risk. "I met a very sexy engineer at my previous job."

"Can engineers be sexy? That's almost as bad as a tax accountant."

"My dear Grady, that's totally prejudiced."

"My two brothers—one's an engineer and the other's a tax accountant—would kick me for saying that."

That was so typical of Grady, an engineer and an accountant in the family. Except that Grady had hidden depths. "*Everyone*," she emphasized with a titillating whisper, "can be sexy." *Even you*. She didn't say it. But it was there in her words, her tone, the soft little sizzle in *sexy*. "I definitely felt a spark with him."

"Tell me more."

"Oh, I will. He worked in the Manufacturing building. And we didn't have a lot of women in Manufacturing. The ladies' room had showers and lockers, and I used to change over there when I took my lunchtime run."

"I'm sure your engineer imagined you every day in that shower." His deeper tone said Grady was imagining, too.

"Oh, he did more than imagine. One day I heard the door open, and I was actually surprised because no one else ever seemed to use that ladies' room."

"I know where this is going."

"Then I don't need to tell you."

"You're killing me," he whispered. "Give me more."

She felt the desperation, his need and desire, and she didn't care whether it was for the story or for her. "I was drying off."

"Naked?"

She didn't chide him for a question whose answer was so obvious. She knew what he wanted, details. "Completely naked. My skin all glistening and wet. Very wet."

All he gave was one sharp intake of breath.

"And there he was, pushing me back into the shower cubicle. He flipped the curtain closed and he was on me, hauling me against the wall. He devoured me with his mouth, kissing me until I couldn't think." She stopped, her heart racing, a hitch in her breathing. "And then he was in me. It was so fast and so hard and so good. We didn't make a sound, just in case anyone came in, and his mouth never left mine. When we came, we swallowed each other's cries."

"I've never known anyone like you." There was something in the timbre of his voice that might have been reverence.

"When he finished, he told me he hadn't been able to wait until we saw each other after work. That all he could think about was being inside me, and it drove him crazy." She could still remember the heat of those words. There'd been a bit more fumbling than she'd described, the condom, et cetera, but Grady needed the edited version. And quite frankly, that was the version she thought about at night when she needed to release all her pent-up energy.

"You're enough to drive any man crazy."

Did she make him crazy? Or was it just her stories? She was certainly doing something to herself with all her thoughts. She'd completely kicked off the top sheet and shoved all the pillows but one on the floor. Her skin was warm, her body moist, her heart a rapid thump in her chest.

"So that wasn't the first time with him?"

She shook her head, then answered aloud. "No. But it was the only time we took that kind of risk." She worked in HR, after all, and if she'd gotten caught, it would have ended her career. She flirted at work, but she did her actual playing around outside the office. "We enjoyed each other for a couple of months. It was very intense and very fun. I love all the sparks that fly."

"Do you always need to feel a spark?"

"Of course." She wrinkled her brow. "It's not just that a man is good-looking. And well…" She rolled on the bed and cradled the phone close to her ear as if she were laying her head on Grady's shoulder. "There was another guy at that machine shop. He was fairly handsome, but there was just something… I don't know." She sighed. "I was making coffee one morning, and he started rubbing my shoulders. He was standing so close I could feel him over my whole length. And it was just icky. I can't tell you exactly why. But there was some weird ick I'd felt from the moment I met him. So it's not like a guy shows his attraction and boom, it's totally hot. It has to be the right guy doing the right things."

"What makes it the right guy?"

With his voice so close, the darkness intimate around them, her skin bare, it was like revealing her soul to him. "Well, first, he has to make me laugh. Then after that…"

She didn't know. But she thought about why Grady attracted her. "He needs to smell really good. And he has to be smart. Not like a doctorate or anything, just smart about life. And he needs to listen well. He's gotta see things, understand even when I don't say everything out loud." Grady had a way of looking at her, as if he were absorbing every word, as if what she said had importance. It was the first time attraction had happened so long after she'd met a man. But everything was different about Grady.

If he wasn't married…

"How can you let them go after all that intensity?"

She hadn't realized she'd closed her eyes until she snapped them open again. "Because… well…" Because not all men she'd been attracted to had each of those traits. They'd had a couple, while Grady seemed to have them all. "It's like a fantasy. You create it in your own mind. I like to leave before reality hits."

"That's cynical."

"Maybe. But then look at all the failed marriages."

He was silent, and she realized her mistake. "I'm sorry. I didn't mean you. And you're working on your marriage." Except that they were no longer studying Phone Sex 101. This had moved into more intimate territory.

"I called her." He paused. "The way you instructed me to."

"That's good." But if it really was good, why had he called her for the next lesson?

All the sexy softness of his voice was erased as he clipped out, "She's not coming back."

"It's only been two weeks. Give her time."

Again, that hard grate clipped his words. "She left work with her lover."

"Oh." Was he sure? Could he have mistaken what he saw?

His next line answered the question. "She had a drink with me and reiterated that I'm not what she wants. He is."

"Grady, I'm sorry."

"So I need my lessons. I need to know how to do it right. I need to know how to make a woman laugh, how to seem smart for her, how to understand her without her having to tell me, how to show her how badly I want her. How to make her crazy enough to let me do her in the women's restroom at work."

He stole her breath. It was almost as if he were talking about her rather than his wife. "You're doing pretty good so far."

"Enough to win the woman I want?"

"I don't know." There was more to fifteen years of marriage than the things he'd told her. There was history you had to get past as well.

His voice dropped once more to a whisper. "Then teach me everything I need to know."

"Grady."

"Touch yourself for me."

Her blood thrummed through her veins, a hot rush charging her entire body. "What?"

"Phone sex. Isn't that what it's about? You touch yourself and make us both crazy with your sounds, make me desperate for you, make you desperate for me."

"Yes, but—"

"Let my voice make you crazy. Make me feel how badly I want you. Make me dream about you all night long."

Oh yeah, there was something totally different about him. His wife had a lover. She didn't want him back. And for a little while, Jordana could pretend he was desperate for her instead of the wife who had cheated on him.

"Touch yourself for me." He ached to hear her voice, the seductive sound of her desire. He hadn't figured out what Darlene needed, but Jordana was oh so willing to tell him how to fix what he'd done wrong, how to be the man who could make a woman scream. The man a woman thought about when someone else was making love to her.

He needed to make sure Jordana wasn't dreaming of anyone but him, that his voice was the only one she heard in her head.

"Please." He begged. It was what a woman would want, to have a man desperate enough to beg.

Her voice finally whispered across the air into his dark bedroom. "Touch myself where?"

She was telling him what she wanted. He just had to listen, understand, and say the right words. "Touch your nipples. Tell me how it feels."

"They're tight against my fingers. And tender."

"Pinch them for me." It's what he would have done if he'd been stretched out alongside her.

He lay stark naked on his bed, the bed in which he'd made love to Darlene every Saturday night like clockwork. Damn her for taking even this moment from him with the thought of her. He'd pushed the covers to the bottom of the mattress, and the overhead fan blew air across his skin as if fingers trailed his body. Jordana's fingers. Jordana's touch. Not Darlene's.

Jordana gasped. "Oh God, Grady."

His groin tightened to a hard ache at the sound of his name on her lips. "I want you in my mouth. I want to taste your skin, your breasts, tease your nipples until you scream."

Her breath came in hot little pants. He imagined her warmth against his face, the luscious dew of her arousal on his lips.

"Tell me what you want me to do to you." If he was there, he'd already be inside her. But this was so much better. He was harder than he'd ever been, his skin alive with the electric sound of her voice. Every sense was fixed on her. He could even smell her citrus scent made tangier with her arousal. "Tell me," he pushed.

"I want your tongue on me."

"Where?"

"Between my legs."

"Push me down there. Show me what you want. Drag your hands down and spread yourself out for me. Like a feast. Because I want to taste you, sip on you, suckle you."

"Gold star," she gasped out.

"Not yet. No gold star until I make you come."

"*I'm* making me come." She was breathy, seductive, enticing.

"My voice is making you come. You're wet. All slippery. And with your eyes closed, it almost feels like it's my tongue on you."

"Yes." She panted. "Oh God, I've never been so wet or so hot."

"Tell me how good it feels."

"Your voice." A gasp, then a moan. "It's like I can feel your tongue against my ear, all over me, down there, everywhere."

"It is everywhere," he whispered. He flexed his legs, extended his feet. Against his belly, his erection flexed, too. "All over you, licking all your sweet tastes, my fingers in you, teasing, taking, making you crazy."

She cried out his name, and he was sure he heard her climax rolling over her, through the phone, and straight into him.

"The thought of your hands all over your body is making me nuts."

Between quickened breaths, she asked, "Are you hard?"

"Hell, yes." He didn't ask if she'd come. He knew. She hadn't faked it, and she hadn't been thinking of anyone else.

"Then touch yourself for me, too."

He hesitated.

"Do it," she seduced him with a whisper. "I want it."

His sex life with Darlene had generally been enough for him. But Darlene was gone, and this was Jordana. This was Phone Sex 101. This was time to break his clockwork chains. He wrapped his hand around himself and stroked the way he wanted her to do.

"Yes." His voice was like the rasp of sandpaper, harsh and needy.

"Tell me how hard you are for me."

"So hard it hurts. Like I'm going to explode."

"Do you want my mouth on you?"

"Hell, yes."

"Then imagine my lips caressing every inch."

He arched into his hand, and it was her touch, her mouth, her tongue. "Jesus," he hissed.

"You taste so good. All salty sweet."

Her voice made her mouth real as she devoured him. He pulled harder, faster. "Baby." The word just fell out. It wasn't one he used. But then he couldn't stop chanting it to her. "Baby, baby."

"It's so good, isn't it. You love the way I do this. You adore my mouth. You beg me to do this all the time."

Her words, her voice, her mouth, his own fantasies, all of it drove him to the cliff, ready to dive off, dying to. "Jordana, baby, please, God."

He wasn't himself anymore. He wasn't Grady Masterson. He was her slave.

His release shuddered through him. His body jerked and spasmed. He didn't know what he said, but he felt her voice on the inside, stroking him, pushing him higher than he'd ever been.

When he crashed back down, he was alone on his bed, and her voice whispered in the dark, "That was five gold stars."

"I'm actually seeing stars."

"You're going to sleep well tonight."

He felt boneless, like he was part of the bed and would never have to move. "Are you?"

"Mmm," she hummed her pleasure. "You definitely passed Phone Sex One-oh-one."

"Is there a Phone Sex One-oh-two," he asked lazily, completely sated as if he wasn't alone in his bed. Her voice had made the difference. Her release just prior to his had turned up the flames, then she'd ignited him into a conflagration.

"I'd better make my next lesson plan now. Nighty-night, Grady."

Her breathy voice was gone, the air on his phone silent. His hand flopped to the side, releasing the cell and letting it plop to the carpet.

That was sex, or maybe even something more. It wasn't a planned revving of the engine on Saturday night, gearing up, pushing in the clutch, driving home. It wasn't clockwork. It was simply Jordana. She made him crazy.

Even better, he'd made her crazy.

He couldn't say if he'd ever made Darlene crazy. Was it the worst thing to admit that he didn't know? Maybe that's why she left him. Maybe everything she'd said was right. He was clueless.

And she was gone.

So was phone sex with Jordana actually cheating?

CHAPTER EIGHT

At eight o'clock the next morning, Jordana still didn't have a lesson plan. Last night, she'd fallen asleep hearing the echo of Grady's climax. He'd breathed hard, groaned, then he swore. Just one word. But it was a crazy, dying-to-have-you word. And she'd come for him, too, touching herself without control or inhibition, crying out, begging. It had been sex, even if they weren't touching each other, even if they were miles apart. Their voices had brought them right into the same room. He'd made it so much sexier than if she'd been scratching an itch all on her own. He took her to heights she'd never managed herself. His voice, his breath against her ear, and most especially his desire. With her eyes closed, she'd been able to pretend it was his hand and his mouth doing those things to her. And she could swear she tasted him on her lips.

They'd crossed a line. She should have been worried. After all, he was married, and she didn't play with married men. But his wife had thrown him away. She'd even flaunted her lover in front of him.

So it was a line that needed to be crossed, right? Of course it did. His marriage seemed to be over, and Jordana wasn't about to let his self-esteem plummet, too. He *did* know what a woman wanted. He'd proven that last night. He'd said all the right words, done all the right things. More lessons might not even be necessary.

Oh but yes, they were totally necessary. Jordana had started to need them as much as Grady did.

"Morning." Gloria King stood on the opposite side of Jordana's credenza. While a CFO and an executive admin didn't usually socialize, the fact that they'd started with the company the same week had turned them into friends.

"I'm dying for Mongolian barbecue. You up for lunch?" Gloria had gorgeous blond hair that fell like thick strands of silk over her shoulders. If Jordana was the envious type, she could have envied Gloria.

She thought a moment about saying no to lunch. Maybe Grady had a naughty plan for her, texting her to meet him somewhere secluded. God, she sounded like a lovesick goldfish pining for her lover who'd accidentally gotten flushed down the toilet.

Grady was married, even he was a dumped married, so lovesick couldn't come into this.

"Yes." Jordana grinned. "You had me at Mongolian barbecue."

She needed friends. Sure, she had acquaintances, girls she went for a drink with, but thinking about Eddie had made her realize there wasn't a single person she would share everything with. Gloria may or not be that person, but Jordana would never find out if she didn't open up a little. She admired Gloria a lot. She was a CFO, obviously a dedicated career woman. She was the woman Jordana wanted to be, smart, confident, and going places.

They agreed to leave at eleven-thirty to beat the lunch rush.

Her cell phone beeped an hour later. And Jordana's heart leaped when it shouldn't.

The thought of you touching yourself while I'm listening is still making me crazy.

They shouldn't be doing this during work hours, but she couldn't stop herself from texting back. Grady's precise typing made *her* crazy, and she couldn't type her reply fast enough. *A+! But you forgot to ask me what I was wearing last night.*

You were completely naked.

Jordana stared at the phone. *How did you know?*

I imagined you that way.

She couldn't help teasing him. *I always sleep naked.*

You're making me crazy again.

Jordana felt the wild thump-bump of her heart. Sexting had always been fun, but with Grady, it was a new level of excitement, maybe because he was older, an authority figure. She really didn't know. She needed to ask a friend: *So why do you think he intrigues me so much?*

She certainly couldn't say that to Gloria. There was sharing, and then there was oversharing.

"Is that a personal text?"

She almost shrieked. Her work came first, yet she hadn't even noticed Rhonda standing on the other side of her short reception wall.

To lie or not to lie.

"Yes." Jordana glanced at her watch and said with a sugar-sweet smile. "But I'm on my break right now." Not really a lie because the timing was right. But she shouldn't be sexting at her desk where Rhonda might have come at her from the side instead of the front and seen exactly what she was typing. She would have been busted. *Grady* would have been busted.

She loved her desire addiction, but she'd always kept it in perspective. She'd never been caught at it, not even *almost* caught. Not until Grady.

"Is there something I can help you with?" she asked ever so politely.

Rhonda frowned. "You shouldn't be texting at your desk even if you are on a break. It looks bad. We're Human Resources, after all."

"You're right. It looks bad." She waggled her phone in the air, the screen now blessedly black. "But employees have my number for emergencies, so I really do need it close at hand."

"Fine." Rhonda turned with a snap, her pivot as sharp as a drill sergeant, and stalked back into her office.

Was Rhonda watching her now, her nose for illicit activity suddenly sniffing out Jordana's sexting? Her job was more important than anything. It was an awesome responsibility. She couldn't let it down for a few brief hits of desire. She needed to be careful.

As if he'd seen Rhonda through his open office door, Grady didn't text again. But she was oddly aware of his voice, his moves, his activity. "Ivy, can you find the Hutchins file?" And Ivy calling out to him, "Mr. Hutchins is on the line now, Grady." Jordana knew when he left for meetings, heard his door close when their CEO, Brett Baker, wanted a conference.

It was almost a relief when Gloria dropped by her

cubicle to pick her up for lunch. She could stop watching Grady.

Gloria paid for her lunch, and they were second in line for grilling their Mongolian barbecue. Jordana skipped the meat and poultry and piled her bowl high with vegetables. The server cooked the mixture on a huge griddle, drizzling it with a fragrant sauce that made her mouth water almost as much as Grady did.

Dammit, she seemed to keep comparing everything to Grady.

"You didn't need to pay for lunch, but thanks."

Gloria smiled. "My pleasure." She tasted her first bite. "I need to start making this at home," she said, savoring the mixture she'd carefully chosen. Hers included succulent morsels of beef.

Jordana knew a few basics about Gloria, who would be forty-eight on her next birthday. Jordana could only hope she'd be in as good a shape at that age. Work out, eat right, and don't frown all the time. Divorced five years ago, Gloria didn't have a current boyfriend. Jordana didn't know whether Gloria had ever had a boyfriend since her divorce. Men seemed to be a taboo subject between them. Jordana had never thought much about crossing that barrier of conversation before.

"You actually cook?" Jordana decided to start asking questions. It was the only way they'd get to know each other.

"Don't you?" The restaurant wasn't even close to capacity the way it would be later so Gloria didn't have to yell to be heard.

"I'm pretty much salads and roasted chicken from Costco. Although I do know how to steam vegetables."

Jordana patted her own shoulder in mock kudos.

Gloria shrugged. "It almost seems like a waste to cook for just one, but the alternative is to clog your arteries with fast food."

They talked about healthy alternatives, going vegetarian versus being a carnivore, and a host of other subjects that Jordana couldn't have remembered even two minutes later, until Gloria hit a completely new topic. "You know I've got those interviews next week with the candidates for VP of Marketing." Gloria stared at her plate, whereas usually she looked at you directly with green eyes that most people found particularly penetrating.

"Right," Jordana agreed, trying to anticipate why Gloria had even brought it up. "We've narrowed it down to the top five."

They weren't selling product yet, but they were in trials with several companies, and Marketing was a highly important function in preparing for the product launch. In addition to the two possible candidates that Brett had worked with in the past, Jordana had screened resumes and picked out the top choices, then done phone interviews to narrow the field even more. They'd brought a selection in for interviews with Rhonda, Brett, plus Court Stevens, their Manufacturing VP, and the Customer Service Manager, Hannah Fall. With the top five chosen, next week would be a round robin of interviews with the executive staff which included all the other VPs. From that, hopefully, they'd have a nominee to whom Brett would then make an offer.

"Well," Gloria said, with a slowness in her voice as if she were considering her exact words. "I know one of the candidates. I worked with him in the past. And I'm wondering if I should skip interviewing him. I don't want to bias the choice or anything." Gloria finally looked up, but Jordana couldn't read much in her eyes or on her face.

But Gloria's words were certainly intriguing. "Is this a bad bias or a good bias?" Jordana asked. "Because if there's something wrong with him, we should definitely know right now."

Gloria lightly rubbed her temple. "It's not really good or bad. It's just… you know…"

No, Jordana didn't know. Then she got it. "Oh my God, you dated him."

Gloria finally huffed out the breath she'd probably been holding for ten minutes. "Sort of."

"Did it end badly? Not that I'm prying or anything." Jordana was prying, but only because Gloria brought it up. "Are you afraid you won't be able to work with him?"

"No. It wasn't a real relationship or anything. And yes, I could work with him. I just felt I ought to come clean that I know him and make sure it's not a problem."

"I can talk to Rhonda about it."

Gloria tossed back her hair, and her nostrils flared slightly, like most people's did when they had to talk to Rhonda about something. "I thought if I spoke with you I could avoid mentioning it to her. I don't really feel like broadcasting this."

Jordana realized Gloria was trusting her with the information and relying on Jordana's judgment. "If you don't think there's going to be any conflict, and you're not aware of any malfeasance on his part—"

"God, no, nothing like that. He's very good at his work, and he'd be an asset to the company."

"The only other concern is a conflict in the

management team. You know Brett likes people to work together, not against each other. So can you work with him?"

Gloria's hesitation was so slight as to be the mere time it took to translate thought into words. "I can work with him."

"Then it shouldn't be a problem, and I don't feel like I have to talk to Rhonda about it."

Technically she was supposed to inform Rhonda of *everything*, at least as far as Rhonda was concerned. But Jordana considered this a confidence, and if it didn't impact the work, she didn't feel the obligation. She'd learned a lot of things in the course of her job that she kept confidential, even from Rhonda.

"But you can't keep me in suspense. Who is it?" Since she and Gloria had been hired at the same time, she'd never looked at her resume so she didn't know which companies might be common with any of the five candidates.

"Parker Hunt."

Jordana let her eyes go wide. Interesting. And it should have been obvious. In his midforties, Parker Hunt was totally hot, with dark hair slightly streaked with gray, as if someone had painted a few individual strands with silver. And Gloria had dated him. *Very* interesting. "It's our secret unless you feel like telling anyone else. And Mr. Hunt has the interview itinerary, so it shouldn't be a surprise to him either."

"We're both adults. It'll be fine. But thanks for keeping it to yourself." Gloria went back to her lunch, having stopped eating during the few minutes the conversation had taken.

She'd actually been worried about the situation, Jordana realized. "You didn't have to buy me lunch just to tell me this."

"It was my pleasure, and it was time we got together for another lunch. Besides, I couldn't very well discuss it in your cubicle."

"You're right. Rhonda can sniff out anything." The tables were filling up with people and noise, the air redolent with grilling meats and spices. Luckily, though, there wasn't a single company man or woman, no one to overhear Rhonda's name.

"You should really have an office with all the confidential things you're involved in. And what about the employee files on your computer?"

"They're stored on the server, so even if someone stole my computer, they still couldn't access anything."

Gloria waved her fork. "But someone could see something if you're looking anything up or keying in new data."

Jordana gave Gloria a cockeyed smile. "I've tried all those arguments on Rhonda. Her answer is that they'd actually have to walk around the reception desktop to see anything."

"Andrew's last day is next Friday, and I'm not replacing him so his office is up for grabs."

Andrew was the Accounting supervisor, but after he turned in his resignation, Gloria had decided the department could do without him. She had a controller and two managers (one for General Accounting and one for Finance which included Cost Accounting) and Andrew's position had become redundant.

"Maybe I should mention the possibility to Rhonda,"

Gloria mused.

"No," Jordana was quick to say. "A woman has to fight her own battles."

Still holding her fork aloft, its tines pointed at Jordana, Gloria said, "All right. But you need to go to battle before someone else puts dibs on it."

Jordana usually took the easiest route, doing things she knew to be right without mentioning them to Rhonda, circumventing her rather than telling her, finding a work-around rather than prompting a confrontation. "It's just that everything with her is a battle."

Gloria shrugged and made a face. "So pick which one you want to fight."

There were so many. She wanted a title other than Administrative Assistant. She wanted an office so she didn't have to keep going to the conference room for all her employee meetings. She wanted to send out employee statistics herself, with her name on the reports, instead of Rhonda always taking the monthly glory.

She didn't want to have to feel guilty about a few personal texts during company time when she usually worked nine to ten hours a day and rarely took a lunch. "By God, you're right. I'm going to push one more time."

"Here-here." Gloria jabbed the air with her fork as if it were a knight's lance. "Run it up the chain of command. You've got my complete support."

"I just need to find the right moment so she doesn't have a chance to shut me down."

It felt pretty darn good, not only making the decision to confront Rhonda, but being the one Gloria chose as her confidant. Jordana wondered if she could actually reveal her emotions about Grady. She wouldn't use his name, of course. She didn't even have to say she worked with the man. She could simply mention the surprise attraction, the way she'd suddenly noticed him after knowing him for so many months, about his almost ex-wife, about the sexting and the phone sex, about thinking of him way too often. Just girl talk and advice.

It was on the tip of her tongue, the words begging to come out. But she hadn't told anyone anything important about herself in so long, and now she wasn't sure she remembered how. What would Gloria think if she mentioned the words *married man*? No, Jordana would have to hold too much back. It was better to keep it all to herself, less risky that way.

She realized she was doing what she always did, relegating the relationship to the surface area. Under the circumstances—Grady being the circumstance—what was the alternative?

CHAPTER NINE

He'd had phone sex with Jordana every night for almost a week, since the evening Darlene told him she'd dreamed about other men when they made love.

Sexting with Jordana hadn't stopped either. He felt alive, every cell on fire, every nerve pinging in anticipation of her answers. It was like a drug during his lunch hour or after office hours ended, until he could get home at night to mainline on phone sex with her.

That was what he'd lost with Darlene, this alive feeling. She was right. He'd lived by the clock, home at seven, eat dinner, answers emails, watch TV, bed by eleven, sex on Saturdays. It was so routine, it was terrifying. He'd driven her into the arms of Mr. GQ's Brooks Brothers suit. And now he was having to learn everything when it was all too late.

But he craved this sense of being utterly alive. He wanted Jordana to show him more, to make him *feel* more.

The building was now empty at the end of the day, and he wanted to get down and dirty.

He actually had his phone in his hand to send the message when it rang. He at first thought the caller was Darlene, and his heart did a strange flip in his chest. He wasn't exactly sure whether he wanted it to be her or he didn't. Fifteen years of marriage ruled his perceptions, and he hadn't been able to shift them to his new reality.

When he looked, it was his mother. Which was worse.

"Darling," he answered. His mother loved endearments.

"Sweetie. How are you?" His mother was a happy sixty-seven-year-old. While she'd loved his dad, and they all still missed him since losing him to a heart attack ten years ago, Mom had never been one to wallow in grief. She was active in her church, organizing bake sales, antique shows, the food bank, and anything that could help the needy. She still walked five miles a day, watched her weight, and had quit smoking so she didn't "pop off without a by-your-leave" as their dad had. Family was everything to her.

"I'm fine, thanks, Mom. What's up?"

"I called Darlene to let her know what to bring for dessert on Sunday, but she doesn't answer. I've left a couple of messages."

Damn. The family dinner every second Sunday of the month, like clockwork. Maybe that was where all his clockwork came from, his mother and her routines.

"She's been really busy at work, Mom." And since she didn't cook, Darlene's offerings had always been store-bought. His mom had suffered through, believing that Darlene wanted to contribute in some small way like all the women in the family did. "I don't think she'll be able to make it for dinner on Sunday." Darlene was probably putting her hands together in a prayer of thanks that she didn't have to attend another Sunday dinner. If she'd thought of anything besides Mr. GQ.

He couldn't say the lie just slipped out without thought. He was being entirely thoughtful when he decided he wasn't ready to talk about Darlene, her divorce email, or the other man. He didn't want the endless questions or have to explain what had gone wrong. He didn't even want the comfort and sympathy he knew his mother would offer. Nor did he feel like blaming Darlene.

"Oh, dear. They're working her even on Sunday?"

"You know how the investment business goes. Any downturn in the market becomes a huge upheaval. Clients need reassurance, portfolios need rebalancing." He was going overboard and shut up.

"That's just too bad. But you'll still be able to come."

"Actually, I thought I'd catch up on some work since she'll be out." His mother would probably read something in the lines of his face. Or one of his brothers would start nagging.

"But you still need to eat, sweetie."

"Mom."

"You're my oldest. I need you there to keep your brothers in line."

He choked back a laugh at her obvious manipulation. "All right, I'll be there." And he'd figure out a way *not* to discuss Darlene's absence. He'd have to tell his mother everything eventually, but he'd rather do it when things were a little more settled.

Right. Like a few days or a week or a month was going to make a difference. Darlene thought of another man while her husband made love to her. Nothing was going to change that.

Unless Jordana showed him exactly what women wanted.

He chatted with his mom for a few more minutes, which, unfortunately, killed all desire to send a dirty, filthy text.

Shrugging on his suit jacket, he shoved his phone in his pocket. He didn't know if Jordana was still here. There wasn't a sound outside his office as he closed his door.

Until her soft seductive voice trickled down his spine. "Fibbing to your mother now, are you?"

He leaned on her reception desk, looking down at her. The position was good, affording him a delicious showcase of her breasts in another of her low-cut tops. Jordana had succulent cleavage. "A little fib is all right when it saves a person's feelings."

She smiled, a luscious curve of her lips that made him want to sip from them.

That's what Jordana did, turned his thinking upside down and inside out. One minute he was lying to his mother and cursing Darlene, then he couldn't drag his gaze out of Jordana's cleavage or squash the image of her lush lips beneath his and her taste exploding on his tongue.

He towered over her as she leaned forward, elbows on her desk, fingers laced. Did she know what that did to him? "That sounds like something your mother taught you."

He laughed. Even her humor was sexy. "Actually she did. She's always believed in little white lies."

She raised her eyebrows. "So who are you protecting? Your mother or your wife?"

"I could say it was my wife."

"You could." She propped her chin on her hand and gazed up at him. "But you're a chicken. You're trying to put off all the inevitable explanations."

It didn't even bother him that she'd read him like the bad lines of a movie script where the hero is actually a wimp. "You got it."

"Just tell her your wife cheated. That says it all."

All his humor faded. "Does it?"

"Of course. You're the wronged party."

"I'm the angry party," he said. "And when you're angry, you don't always see everything clearly."

She stood, as if she couldn't be leered at when they were talking seriously. "That doesn't put her in the right and you in the wrong." She backed up to her desk drawer that contained all her personal paraphernalia.

"It just means that there's always two sides to every story."

Her purse now in hand, she held it to her abdomen as she hammered right to the point. "So you forgive her?"

He answered honestly, because she'd inspired honesty from the very first moment she'd revealed what women really wanted, what *she* wanted. "I don't know. But that's irrelevant. She's got another man in her bed, and I don't feel like opening the whole thing up to family dissection. That's why I lied."

"Fibbed," she corrected softly.

"Told a white lie," he agreed. "I'll walk you to your car." A gentleman just like Mr. GQ. Even if he'd known the guy's name, he would still call him that.

"Thanks."

They were silent in a silent building, not a sound until

her high heels hit the lobby tile downstairs.

It felt oddly good to have confessed the truth.

"Gloria thinks I should petition Rhonda to take over Andrew's office after he leaves," she said in a strange change of topic. "What do you think?"

Andrew's office was in the corner on the opposite side from Grady's, and he didn't like that he wouldn't be able to see her every time he walked out his door. Of course, he couldn't say that. "With the confidentiality of your job, it makes sense to have your own office."

"All the employee files are in Rhonda's office so they can be locked up. But I use them a lot more than she does."

Down in the lobby, he pushed the outer door open for her and made sure it latched properly when it closed behind them. "It's a good move. She should have figured that out already."

"I'll talk to her tomorrow."

They approached her car. His was on the other side of the lot. "Goodnight," he said.

"Goodnight," she answered, digging in her purse for her keys.

She beeped her remote as he headed for his own car. They hadn't talked about phone sex, sexting, or his next lesson. There'd only been room for Darlene and his little white lie.

He was a couple of parking spots away when he turned. Opening her door, she threw her purse across to the passenger seat. A light evening breeze picked up her hair, blowing it gently, prettily. Her legs were long and toned beneath the short black skirt she wore.

He didn't think, he simply acted. In four long strides,

he was on her. Grabbing her arm, he hauled her close, a breath whooshing out of her. Then her lips were beneath his.

Her mouth opened, and her taste was tangy and sweet as her citrus scent. He enveloped her with both arms, the press of her breasts against him, her cherried nipples as tight and hard as she'd described to him every night. He sank into her, teasing the recesses of her mouth, her tongue flirting with his. Then he growled in his throat and devoured her, taking the kiss deep. He tasted her moan, felt it vibrate against him, inside him. The fire in her lips consumed him, engulfed them both. She trembled in his arms. His blood roared in his ears and pulsed in his fingertips where he touched her. He flared to life like a lit match, burning hot, until they were both breathing fast, gasping, and he pulled back just to make sure he hadn't lost his mind, that she was real.

"Oh my dear James," she said on a puff of air. "Now *that* was a kiss."

He hadn't meant to emulate the kiss or the actor. He simply dove on her, took what he needed, what he craved, what he couldn't live without for one more second.

He gulped air and stepped back, suddenly remembering they were in a parking lot across the street from the factory building which ran two shifts. Even if the company headquarters was empty, Manufacturing wasn't. And he wasn't about to jeopardize her reputation.

"Gold star?" he asked to dilute the moment and some of his emotion. His body was still hard, his skin still on fire, his breath still lost to her.

She nodded. Her lipstick was gone but her mouth was lush and swollen with his kiss. He wanted it again, wanted to lean in, plunder…

"What's my next lesson?" He had to have one, would die if it all ended now.

"Ummm…"

"Don't tell me you haven't got a lesson plan."

"Role-play," she said quickly as if she'd only just decided. He counted the beats of silence before she added, "At a bar. So it's better if we do it on Friday."

"What kind of role-play?"

She wagged her finger at him. He wanted to suck it into his mouth and taste her skin. "I'll give you the details over the next couple of days."

She was winging it. He didn't care. Whatever she did, she'd make it good.

He'd never given up so much control to a woman before. He was letting her lead, make all the moves, determine the direction. It was the hottest thing he'd ever done. There was no clock ticking telling him when; there was just desire pulling him under.

She got in her car. "I'll text you tomorrow." Then she closed the door and started her engine. His was already racing.

Like a love-struck zombie, he didn't move until her car bumped out of the parking lot and its taillights disappeared around the corner.

She'd started it all by telling him what a woman needed was to feel desired. He was aching with desire, on edge with it, close to crazed. And he freaking loved the feeling, his body on fire, all his neurons exploding.

This was what he hadn't delivered on with Darlene from the moment their lovemaking had turned into clockwork. This was what she got from Mr. GQ, wild and crazy. It was like a drug.

The problem was she'd gotten hooked on a different man's drug. Grady wasn't sure he could change that now.

He wasn't sure he even wanted to. All he could think about was Jordana's next text, Jordana's next lesson. Jordana's next kiss.

She stopped at the light and put her fingers to her lips. They still tingled. Jordana could still taste him, man and sex and desire filling her mouth, tantalizing her mind.

He was better than the Bridget Jones kiss, or even *Becoming Jane* and *Penelope*.

She hadn't expected the rush, but the moment he touched her, put his lips on her, hauled her up in his arms, she'd tumbled down into him.

He was crazy good. She was just plain crazy. He'd lied to his mother about his wife. He'd begged for lessons on how to make his wife desire him. Everything was about his wife. For God's sake, she'd dumped him by email only three weeks ago.

And stupid Jordana was falling. Not in love, of course—because she wasn't stupid enough to do *that*—but in complete and total lust. They didn't have a relationship, but falling in lust could still hurt when it ended. Especially if his wife realized what an absolute idiot she was for cheating on such a delicious, marvelous man.

The light changed and someone honked before she even had a chance to put her foot on the accelerator.

There was a metaphor in that, she was sure.

She was letting herself get deeper than she should, faster than she should. This time she was more than a desire junkie, she was a desire junkie for *him*. Even if they weren't in a real relationship, it could get messy. She worked right outside his office. If he ended their lessons before she was ready, she'd still have to see him every day, a *million* times a day.

She felt herself spiraling down, circling the drain, and she jerked herself up.

He'd kissed her. It was fabulous. It was stupendous. It was downright breathtaking and body sizzling. But it was just a kiss. She was still in control. All she had to do was keep reminding herself. Because she wasn't ready to stop, nowhere near.

So, step one, think of a really sexy role-play for Friday night. Step two, send him a bunch of texts that would drive him absolutely nuts over the next two days. Okay, okay, some of them would be during workhours, but she'd make them quick. Step three, make sure she got that corner office, just in case she couldn't bear to see Grady a million times every day after their lessons were over. Oh, and because she needed that office due to the confidential nature of her work.

Grady hadn't called her last night. It was as if that kiss had trumped Phone Sex 101. Talk was no longer enough. It was terrifying yet exhilarating. Just as they had while she was driving home, her lips tingled as she watched him arrive the next morning, unlock his door, remove his suit jacket. Then he simply turned and looked at her a long moment through the office door.

And she knew he was thinking about the kiss, too. It sizzled in the air between them.

She could have gazed at him all day. But Ivy arrived, her short, dark bob a bit of a mess, as if she hadn't found time to even run a brush through it. She whispered to Jordana a mile a minute about her little girl getting a summer cold at daycare and how she'd begged her mother to take her in for a couple of days. Jordana felt for the difficulty of being a single working parent. She didn't want that for any kid she might have. She knew too well what it was like, her flaky dad gone when she was three, and her mom not caring a whole lot about leaving her alone after Jordana was the age of ten, like turning ten was a magic number that deemed her totally self-sufficient.

When she looked up again, Grady had retreated to his desk and was already making calls.

So Jordana tackled step three of the plan she'd made up last night in the car. Since her lunch with Gloria last week, she'd been looking for just the right moment to work on Rhonda. She was starting to realize there would never be a right moment, and if she wasn't careful, Andrew would be gone and the office would go to someone else.

"You don't need an office." Rhonda didn't even look up from the stack of resumes Jordana had laid on her desk.

Jordana had already screened them. All Rhonda had to do was tick a yes-or-no box. Jordana knew from experience that Rhonda would say yes to everyone, and Jordana would start the phone interviews.

"Are you aware how many times I have to retreat to

the conference room for confidential conversations I can't have in my cubicle?"

Rhonda ticked a box. "Good. It's like an office for you then."

"All the physical files I need to work with are in your office."

Rhonda ticked another box. She hadn't had enough time to even read the resume. "You're welcome to them any time."

"I constantly work on confidential material on my computer."

Rhonda smiled at the next box she ticked off and the next resume she put on the completed pile. "That's why your computer faces away from prying eyes."

She asked the only question that needed answering. "Why don't you want me to have an office, Rhonda?"

"This has nothing to do with me *not* wanting you to have an office."

It had to do with Rhonda wanting to keep her in her place. "Andrew's office will be vacated tomorrow." Jordana would conduct his exit interview at one o'clock on Friday, after his going-away lunch. He'd be free to take his box of personal items out to his car and drive off into the sunset. "There are no new hires to fill it."

Rhonda sighed and finally laid down her pen. "Jordana, it's a fact of life that administrative assistants don't get offices." She flicked a hand off to the left in the general direction of Andrew's small office. "Besides, I need you right here where you're readily available."

Where she was at Rhonda's beck and call. Jordana flicked her hand in imitation. "You have a second door right here. You'll be able to see me." Rhonda had two entrances, but only the other VPs used the second one. Everyone else had to go through Jordana.

Rhonda leaned back to look out that door. "I can only see the corner of the desk through the glass beside the door."

This had become the most ridiculous argument. "It doesn't matter if I'm an executive admin, because employee confidentiality is at risk. It doesn't matter whether you can see me or the corner of my desk or anything at all, because you can pick up the phone and call me when you need something."

Her lips pursed, Rhonda made a wide-eyed irritated face. "It won't fly with the executive committee."

It would if they thought someone might find out their salaries and bonuses. "Would you like me to ask them? I can send out an email. Let's do a poll." She put a finger to her chin and looked up at the corner of the office. "Dear Executive Staff, are you worried that *your* confidential information isn't as secure as it should be?"

Rhonda huffed out a big breath that blew the remaining resumes across her desk. "All right. Fine. I'll ask at the next staff meeting."

That would on Monday. Jordana didn't trust Rhonda to actually bring it up, but one very convenient duty she had was to make up the meeting's agenda and email it to all the executives. She'd be sure to put her item on there. "Thank you, Rhonda."

First, she'd acquire an office. Then she'd go to work on a promotion to HR supervisor.

She was pleased with herself. Her reward would be a short break so she could send Grady the first of her texts about their role-play tomorrow night.

CHAPTER TEN

Jordana was doing a good job of keeping him in suspense. By the time Friday night's role-play was only half an hour out, all Grady knew for sure was the time and place, but she'd tantalized him with sexts of all her different scenarios. Not knowing exactly what she'd do had driven him a little nuts. He could taste her all over again, reliving that kiss in the parking lot until his body was drumming with desire. He hadn't called her late at night, though he'd wanted to badly enough that he ached with the need to hear her voice, to listen to the soft purr of her moans. But that kiss. It had changed something. If he'd talked to her on the phone, he would have ended up begging her to let him come over.

Jordana had chosen a bar on University Avenue in Palo Alto. That, of course, meant it would be as crowded as hell on Friday evening after work, accompanied by the risk that someone from the office might see them.

There was also the much bigger risk that Darlene would be the one to catch them, since she worked just around the corner. Let her come. Three weeks ago, she'd dumped him. Whatever he did now wasn't her business. Unless she wanted to change her mind. And he doubted that.

The only thing that truly interested him was Jordana's latest text. His phone chirped, and he read her next instruction. He was to find a seat at the bar. And wait.

Grady was a patient man. The crowd was mostly suits, the women in skirts and blouses, several more buttons undone than would have been office regulation. He elbowed through the throng, suffering a few jabs to his solar plexus, and snagged the last seat at the bar. Luckily most people were waiting for tables, not a single bar stool.

He ordered a beer, shouting to make himself understood. It still required a bit of pointing, too, indicating the beer on tap. The noise level was painful, echoing in the high ceilings. Tables were wedged in like the little cheeses that came in a pack. A bar stool ended up on his foot, but he wore a thick pair of dress shoes and didn't suffer any damage. The air conditioning wasn't up to the overpopulated task, and his nostrils were assailed by end-of-day sweat spritzed with an extra layer of presumably manly cologne that was supposed to mask it. But the beer was good and the mug frosty.

He shifted on his stool as a young woman squeezed into the small space between him and another man's back.

"Hi," she shouted at him. "You don't mind if I just get a beer, do you?"

He signaled permission with his hand. She was attractive, her dark hair pulled back in a ponytail, and her black-and-white striped bra showing through her white, short-sleeved shirt. Only the young. In his day, women didn't flaunt their underwear like it was a fashion accessory.

In his day. Hell, he sounded like his long-dead grandfather.

His phone jumped on the bar. If he hadn't put it on vibrate, he never would have heard it, but as it was, the thing shimmied across the wood until he grabbed it up.

Are you flirting with that hussy?

His gaze darted around the wall-to-wall crowd, but he couldn't spot Jordana.

He typed back. *She's trying to steal my seat at the bar.*

That's encouraging. Try to pick her up.

He grimaced. *She's young enough to be my daughter.*

The topic of conversation was smiling at him with big white teeth and very red lipstick.

His phone vibrated in his hand. *Girls her age love older men. The daddy syndrome.*

"Your wife texting you to find out when you'll be home?"

How did she know he was married? Then he remembered his wedding ring. He hadn't taken it off, not even after the night in the bar with Darlene when she told him she thought about someone else when he made love to her. The ring was like an appendage, part of him. It had been there so long he didn't even notice it. The thought made his stomach clench. Didn't that say a lot about his marriage? Maybe Darlene wasn't totally wrong when she complained he was complacent.

He'd think about all that later. Right now, the ring worked in his favor. Grady moved just his eyes to look at the young woman. "Actually, she's texting to say she's working late."

"Ooh," she pursed her lips. "Bad sign."

Why was it taking this girl so long to order her beer? The barman had attended to him in a matter of minutes. Yet now he was at the other end of the bar filling a huge drink order for one of the tables.

"A bad sign of what?" His phone buzzed, and he glanced down to read the continuing text conversation. *She's pursing her lips like she wants to kiss you. This is going well.*

"No one works late on a Friday night. She's going out for a drink with someone." She blinked dark eyelashes at him. Her makeup was expertly done, making her eyes sultry, her cheekbones high, and her lips quite kissable. *If* she was Jordana.

This wasn't the role-play he wanted. And the young woman actually had the nerve to remind him about Darlene and all the Friday nights she'd worked late.

"Well, at least that gets you off the hook." She batted her thickly mascaraed eyelashes. "Now you can do whatever you want without being afraid you'll get caught."

Her insinuation irked him. "What makes you think I'm not meeting my wife here?"

She laughed as prettily as a spider. "This is a pick-up place."

"Are *you* picking someone up?" he asked.

She turned fully toward him. He was almost sure she hadn't even signaled the bartender yet. "Maybe I'm trying to pick you up."

"You're joking." His phone buzzed again. He held it up right in front of the girl's face so he could read it.

You're definitely making progress. She's 100% focused on you.

He wanted to put his fingers to his temple. Where the hell was Jordana?

"I like older men." The young woman smiled at him, all teeth. Shark teeth.

"How old are you?"

She tilted her head coquettishly. "Twenty-two."

"I'm forty-two."

"Perfect. You remind me of my boss. I adore authority figures."

He stopped in mid-thought, turning his head slightly to assess her from the corner of his eyes. "She sent you over, didn't she?"

She brought her eyebrows together in a little furrow. "Who?"

"This is some sort of game you two cooked up."

"You mean a ménage?"

He spluttered before finally coming out with, "You're too young to know what a ménage is."

This was Jordana's role-play? A ménage with her and a girl young enough to be his daughter?

"Of course I know what a ménage is. I have streaming."

"But have you ever been part of a ménage?" He honestly wanted to know. It would completely blow his dress shoes off his feet if she said yes. Then again…

"No. But it's one of the things on my bucket list."

He felt a frown form on his forehead. "Your bucket list?"

"Things I want to do before I die."

"But you're only twenty-two."

"I fully expect to expand my bucket list the older I get. But you can never start too early because who knows if your destiny is to be run over by a bus when you're only twenty-three." There wasn't the hint of a twinkle in her eye or a line of humor on her lips. She was completely serious.

"I don't have a bucket list."

She leaned her elbow on the bar top, and her eyes started to sparkle as she asked him, "What would you put on it if you had to write one tonight?"

Jordana chose that moment to text him again. "Excuse me. I think my wife is confirming that she's going to be here soon."

Instead Jordana's text said: *She looks like she's settling in for the long haul. Are you propositioning her?*

He didn't even bother looking for her. She'd probably gotten here early and taken a seat behind one of the wooden posts holding the ceiling up.

He typed his reply. *She wants a ménage. Are you up for it?*

"What did you tell her?" The girl tried to peer over his arm at his phone.

"I told her you wanted a ménage and asked if she was game."

Her eyes went wide. "Get out. You didn't."

He scrolled so that only his text was visible, then turned it for the young woman to read.

"Oh. My. God." She practically squealed, but of course it was so loud in the place no one could hear her. "Are you two swingers?"

"I think swinging implies we switch partners. But since you don't have one..." He let the sentence hang.

"What does she look like?"

"Very hot. Absolutely gorgeous with nut-brown hair past her shoulders, striking blue eyes, and killer curves." He had no idea why he was leading her on, except that it had suddenly become fun.

"Is she bi?" She seemed to be vibrating at the same

speed his phone did when one of Jordana's texts came in.

"We haven't explored that yet. So it might just be the two of you pleasuring me."

She guffawed and put her hand over her mouth as if the sound had surprised her. "I fooled around a little bit with my college roommate. So I wouldn't mind if you watched me and your wife get a little nasty together."

He really was backward. He worked hard, came home, answered emails, watched TV, and engaged in clockwork sex. Who could possibly have known there was so much more out there? No wonder he couldn't satisfy Darlene. He'd even had to ask Jordana, who was twelve years younger, to give him lessons on what a woman wanted.

His hand vibrated. Jordana had taken so long to reply that he'd figured he'd shocked even her.

You have once again exceeded all expectations.

The young lady was bobbing on her high heels. "What did she say?"

"That I've exceeded expectations."

"Do you guys do this all the time? I'm a psychology student and this is like so interesting."

He held up a finger, then typed. *What am I supposed to do with her now?* Then he gave the girl a halfway honest answer. "This is our first time."

"Wow."

"But we could be a couple of serial killers trying to lure an unsuspecting young lady back to our hotel room where we'll torture and then dismember you."

Her mouth dropped open. Then she laughed. "That's a joke, right. You're a very funny man." She put her finger in the middle of his chest.

Grady actually recoiled, bumping into someone behind him.

"So where would we go to do this thing?" she wanted to know.

He held up his finger again, forcing her back as he typed with his other thumb.

Rescue me.

Jordana hadn't realized the bar would be quite so jammed and though she'd arrived early to secure a table, the only one left was around the corner of the bar and back near the bathrooms. If she leaned out just a bit, she could see him.

He was amazing. The man claimed he didn't know a thing about women, but the little hottie had zeroed in on him within five minutes.

While Jordana had teased Grady with several sexy role-plays where he'd have to be assertive and make her feel so desired that her panties would be damp with need, her choice had been for them to pretend they were strangers. And he would have to pick her up. A simple, basic role-play to start him off with. Of course, she'd play terribly hard to get.

Yet there he was at the bar attended to by a sexy little nymph all the other solo men—meaning they weren't with a date though that didn't necessarily make them single—were drooling over. And she'd jumped Grady.

A ménage. How did that come up? Yes, he was truly amazing. But now he needed rescuing.

Jordana gave up her table, which was immediately dived upon by no less than six business-attired men, and headed Grady's way.

She was at his back when she heard the younger woman say with a tinkle of laughter, "Is this the other serial killer?"

Grady swiveled on his bar stool. "Darling," he said, fright making his eyes wide as he wrapped his arm around her, pulling her close as if she were a shield.

"Serial killer?" She eyed them both. "What has he been getting up?"

The young brunette flapped a hand at her. "He said you two could be serial killers trying to lure victims up to your hotel room for a little torture and dismemberment."

Jordana started to laugh, then couldn't stop. Grady had to wipe the tears from beneath her eyes. She liked his arm around her and loved the tender touch on her face.

"God, that made me thirsty," she told him. "Can I have some of your beer?"

He handed her the mug and she drank greedily. "He is such a card," she finally managed to say.

"He was right." The girl was smiling. Obviously the serial killer thing hadn't scared her away. "You do have killer curves. And you're totally gorgeous."

Jordana palmed Grady's cheek, feeling oddly warm despite the cold beer. "Did you really say that about me, sweetie?"

He scooched her closer, if that was even possible since she was already plastered to his side. "I told her the absolute truth."

Wednesday night's scorching kiss had been a demonstration that he'd learned every trick out of the chick flicks. And tonight was role-play. She could do anything she wanted, maybe even everything she wanted.

"That was so nice." She cupped his face in both hands and put her lips to his in a long, lingering kiss. He opened his mouth and she teased his tongue. Turning her head, she took him deeper, savoring him with a long, sweet taste. The kiss was heady, and heat blossomed inside her, melting her against him.

"Hey, you two, get a room." Then the young woman leaned in to say, "And let me come with you." Her gaze was eating them up, while Grady's eyes were a bit dazed.

He nuzzled Jordana's hair and whispered, "Do that again."

Jordana wanted to fall right into him. Her hands held his face still, and her lips were only a kiss away. A little voice in her head chanted, *More, more, more.*

"You two are just so cute," their little friend went on. "Not like most married couples."

She was a dose of reality. They didn't act like married people because they weren't married. At least not to each other. And Grady still had that wedding ring on his finger. She wanted to forget that part. His gaze almost did make her forget it.

"Most married people don't even talk except for stuff like 'please pass the mashed potatoes' or 'please take out the garbage in the morning.'"

"That sounds pretty polite to me." Even as she talked to the brunette, Jordana clung to Grady. Or he was clinging to her. However it happened, their arms were wrapped around each other like they were one unit.

"You're right, they wouldn't use the word *please.*" The girl gave a mock scowl that maybe wasn't so mock. Her parents must have been great role models for marital bliss. She leaned in, all wide-eyed interest. "So tell me, is your secret to happiness that you have sex with other people?"

Grady started to laugh then, and Jordana buried her face against his shoulder. He smelled so good, felt so good, and his laughter made her tingle as much as his body heat did.

"Okay, you two, I can't take anymore," he said, still chuckling even as he got himself under control. He lifted Jordana's chin. "Where do you come up with these ideas?"

"Which idea?"

He pointed at the pretty brunette. "Her."

She pulled his finger down. "It's not polite to point."

"Sorry." But he chuckled again anyway.

"So, are we going to do this thing or not?" The girl was so young, so fresh, despite the expertly yet heavily applied makeup.

"Do what?" Jordana asked.

She huffed dramatically, but with a bright twinkle in her big brown eyes. "The ménage," she mouthed.

The place was a crush of bodies and loud with so many voices you couldn't make out anything that was said beyond a foot away. Thank goodness there wasn't music as well or no one would hear anything. In this case, that might have been a good thing. Because she could definitely read the girl's lips.

Jordana let herself fall into the role. Turning fully into Grady's arms, she stood between his spread legs. Her hands links behind his neck, she cooed at him. "What do you think, sweetie?"

He hauled her closer, tighter, until she could feel the hard length of him. "Right now, the only thing I can think about is getting you out of that skirt."

Her heart tripped all over itself as if he wasn't simply playing his assigned role.

"That kiss made me crazy," he whispered. "You make me totally wild."

His mouth closed over hers in a hard fast kiss that suddenly made her spin. She might have slid right to the floor if he wasn't holding her up, but it was over way too soon.

"You said you wanted your man desperate for you, can't get enough of you, his hands all over you."

If they'd been alone, she was sure Grady's hands would have been everywhere. His eyes hypnotized her, his touch seduced her, and his lips said the prettiest, sexiest things.

"So do you want me?" he said against her mouth before he pulled back. "Or a ménage?"

Their eyes locked, she felt his heartbeat beneath her fingertips, hard and fast, just like his kiss had been. There was only one answer. "You."

He looked at the girl. "Sorry. No ménage. No torture. No dismemberment." He rose from the bar stool and grabbed Jordana's hand.

"Wow," their friend enthused. "I want to be like you two when I grow up. Married sex. That is just so hot."

"Oh yeah," Grady called over his shoulder as he muscled his way through the crowd, pulling Jordana with him. "Totally hot."

She felt utterly desired, as if this gorgeous man couldn't wait one more second to have her. He pulled her along the sidewalk, around the corner toward one of the parking lots, then around the corner of the building, and shoved her up against the wall. His body suddenly plastered to hers, he devoured her lips until she couldn't breathe. The kiss was hard and needy, testing all the recesses of her mouth. He was relentless, teasing her with his tongue, then consuming her, his body pressed hard against her until she couldn't harbor a single doubt about how badly he wanted *her*, not some woman who had divorced him by email. He shoved his fingers into her hair and held her head so he could sip every pleasure he wanted from her, feast on her. She'd never felt sexier, never felt more desired. If they'd been alone, she'd have let him do anything.

"I want to come home with you." His voice was a rasp against her lips just before he devoured her again.

CHAPTER ELEVEN

God yes, please. She'd never wanted anything as much as this. She was a desire junkie, but Grady was now the only drug that could work on her. His kiss was a long, luscious melding of their mouths, their mingled breaths, his taste fresh and foamy like the beer. She was parched for more of him. Fisting her hands in his suit jacket, she wanted to press every inch of him against her. She wanted skin beneath her touch.

When they finally surfaced to the warm night air around them, a car door slamming, high heels on the pavement, voices, she had to laugh just to break the spell.

"I declare that you've officially graduated from the Jordana Davis School of What Women Want." Oh God, she wanted, so badly she ached in the deepest, most secret part of her.

Grady, still breathing hard, didn't back off. "That was just Kissing One-oh-one. What about the rest of my classes?"

Touching 101. Licking 101. Tasting 101. Shoving Her

Up Against the Wall and Lifting her Skirt 101. And so much more. She wasn't sure she'd survive Putting Your Hand Between Her Legs 101, let alone Making Her Come 101.

And this from a desire junkie!

She pushed at him just so she could drag in a complete breath. "Triple A-plus for Kissing One-oh-one. I'll have to decide what's next on the agenda."

"Take me home with you," he said softly. "Teach me now."

It completely terrified her. He was so serious, his gaze burning into her, his touch sizzling against her skin. "We didn't say we were going to have sex."

He held her against the wall with his hands, his body, and his desire. "No, we didn't."

"It's crossing a line," she told him. As if he couldn't figure that out for himself.

"We crossed that line when I stroked myself and came to the sound of your voice in my ear." His head dropped to her hair and she heard him inhale her scent, taking her deep inside himself.

She swallowed. Why was she fighting? Her body screamed at her to say yes. She was wet, hot, ready. She wanted to taste him in her mouth, feel his body fill hers. She wanted to come with his mouth on her.

"You're married."

He leaned with both hands against the wall above her head. It gave her just a bit more breathing room.

"My wife is divorcing me." He didn't have to add that she was also cheating on him.

She put her palms to the wall, afraid to touch him. "I work right outside your office. It could get very messy."

"It's just lessons," he murmured against her hair.

That's what frightened her. From the moment he flew onto her radar screen, Grady had been different from any other man.

"Teach me how to please you in bed."

His voice, his scent, his lips so close, his body so hard, everything about him made her reckless, wild, and crazy. She wanted it all so badly that her mouth watered and her nipples peaked against the thin material of her shirt.

"I'll follow you home. And if you say no on your doorstep, I'll go away." With that, Grady passed How to Seduce a Woman Out of Her Panties 101. And he got two gold stars as well.

She leaned her head back to meet his eyes. "You make it hard to resist."

His dark gaze bored right into her. "Don't resist."

She didn't say anything for a moment that stretched between them. He didn't break either. "Why?" she finally whispered.

"Your little role-play girl made me realize that a woman doesn't want married sex. She wants crazy sex. She wants wild sex. And I don't even know what that is."

"She wasn't *my* role-play girl." She seemed only able to answer one part of it at a time. He dazed her with his thinking.

"Whatever. You sent her to me. I played along."

"But I didn't send her to you. You did that all on your own. That girl wanted *you.*"

He tipped his head like a retriever waiting for his master to throw the next stick. "You're pulling one over on me. There's no way some young woman is going to walk up and say all that to me."

She puffed out a laugh. "That's exactly what she did. Don't you get it? She totally came on to you. You had her seduced before I even walked over. So you see"—she poked her finger in his chest—"you already know everything you need to know."

He regarded her with a hooded gaze that disguised his feelings. "It's pretty hard to believe. She said everything I needed to hear. She made me realize that I have to know what it's like."

"A ménage?" With all of her naughty tricks, Jordana hadn't tried that one.

He laid his forehead against hers. "No. Not a ménage with her or anyone else. I want only you to teach me about wild, crazy sex."

Her heart started the wild rat-a-tat again. "I have been teaching you. I told you all those stories."

He bracketed her throat with his hand. It was so possessive, so intimate… so sexy and crazy. They were no longer touching anywhere, just his hand on her and the heat between them. She'd taught him that, too. Or he was simply a natural. He already knew what to do, touching her in ways that threatened to melt her resistance like wax on a candle.

"Teach me," Grady whispered, his lips so close that all she had to do was tilt her chin a millimeter and they'd be on hers.

God, she wanted to teach him. She wanted the pleasure, wanted to close her eyes and feel his naked skin against hers, wrap her body around his, wanted the unrelenting wall at her back as he lifted her skirt and took her hard, fast, and high.

All her resistance was suddenly a melted pool at her feet.

"All right. You can follow me home." She didn't add that he'd need to leave if she changed her mind. There was no way she would. Not now.

She wanted Grady Masterson more than she'd wanted any other man.

Grady's hands were tight around the steering wheel as he followed the taillights of her car. He could still taste her, still smell her all over him, that tangy citrus that was uniquely her.

So Jordana hadn't planted the girl as his role-play. She'd found him all on her own. He didn't care a whit whether she'd wanted him or he was just a subject of her sociology degree. The only thing that mattered was that she'd opened his eyes to all the things he'd missed and to his culpability in destroying his marriage through insufficient interest.

And she'd opened his eyes to the fact that he needed Jordana to teach him how to please a woman. She was the only one who could teach him, the only woman he *wanted* to teach him.

He could have taken her right there against the building wall in that parking lot. He would have risked arrest. He would have risked anything except her. The hardest thing he'd ever done was back away, but begging her to teach him had been so easy. He was willing to beg for anything from her.

A woman wanted to feel desired, but Grady realized a man wanted to feel crazy with that desire. His body thrummed, his blood raced, and his skin hummed like a live wire.

When she'd kissed him so naturally in the bar, as if they'd done it a thousand times before, she'd swept him onto some other plane of existence. There was only Jordana. The young woman had made him laugh, but Jordana turned him insane. And he loved it. He was alive. He was in the moment. No past, no future, just this moment with her.

She got on the freeway, and in the deepening twilight, he merged behind her into late rush-hour traffic. She was just a silhouette. He should have made her drive with him. What if she changed her mind?

He was married. He didn't know the rules on cheating. He didn't know if Darlene's defection ended his monogamy or if it was just an excuse to take what he wanted. It didn't change the fact that he was going to make love to Jordana tonight. He was going to give her everything she'd ever described to him.

She exited in Mountain View. He followed right on her tail, turning along the same twisting path of city streets that she did. He was behind her when she pulled into an apartment complex, slowed down to avoid a dog running across the drive, then turned into a numbered parking spot beneath a carport. He found guest parking farther on.

What would he do if she'd changed her mind? He'd already coerced her, but she'd had fifteen minutes to think it over without his voice whispering in her ear.

He thought about taking his suit jacket off and throwing it across the seat. But removing it was like an expectation so he left it on but unbuttoned. Pocketing his keys, he headed back to her carport, waiting by her trunk as she gathered her purse and briefcase and a sweater he'd never seen her wear.

Carrying everything in her arms, she stopped between her car and the next, just looking at him, her expression hidden in shadows.

He'd say anything to convince her. He'd beg all over again. She had that much power over him. But she also had the power to make him realize he'd said everything already. Another word would be one too many.

Jordana didn't say anything at all. She simply brushed past him, reaching out to grab his tie and pull him along with her. And that told him everything he needed to know.

Jordana was shivery with desire, her skin alternately hot and cold. Grady followed her up the stairs to her second-floor apartment and stood so close behind her as she unlocked the door that she could feel his hard, ready body.

"Do you know how much I want you?" he murmured against her hair. "I'm crazy for you."

God, he was perfect, all the right words, actions, everything a woman could ask for.

She closed the door, and he was on her right there in the darkened foyer. Everything she'd been carrying in her arms thudded to the floor as he pinned her against the door. Tunneling his hands beneath her hair, he plundered her mouth.

She was drowning in his kiss, the mastery, the possession. He'd learned all his lessons, unless he'd never really needed them at all. His tongue invaded her mouth, and she savored his taste. It was the bad-boy kiss in *Bridget Jones's Diary*. It was James. God, no, it was Grady, and no one had ever made her head spin the way he did. Her knees weak, she clung to his arms, afraid she'd fall if she didn't hang onto him.

Then he hauled her high until she wrapped her legs around his waist. Her high heels *thunked* on the tile floor as she flipped them off.

"Kiss me," he demanded, his voice harsh with need.

It was a page out of one her stories. Her blood was racing through ever vein and capillary. Her breath came so fast, she felt faint. Fire rushed over her skin. Grady's heart thumped wildly against her as she wound her arms around his neck and lowered her mouth to his. She licked his lips, sucked his tongue, then pulled away to angle her head. Her hair fell around them like a curtain, intensifying their rough breaths, their mingled scents of arousal, his a heady musk of desire. He was hard and insistent between her legs, her body reacting with a rush of moisture and need. She pulled his hair, yanking him closer until she could sink her tongue into him. They played from his mouth to hers, breathing hard, a growl deep in his throat, a moan rising from hers.

This was desire. This was need. This was *I'll die if I don't have you*.

Then he put both hands beneath her butt and rocked into her, mimicking the act, his body like steel against her. She tore her mouth from his, dragging in air, gasping it out, her head back against the door, eyes closed as he buried his face in her hair tangled around her throat. She could come just like this. She could never want for anything more.

"Jesus." His voice was heavy and harsh.

"Grady, please." It was summer. She didn't wear nylons. He could take her right now, right up against the door. All he had to do was unzip and pull her panties aside. "Please," she begged, tightening her legs around him, pulling him deeper, harder.

Wordless, he tugged at her shirt, pulling the neckline aside right along with the lacy cup of her bra. Dipping his head, he sucked her nipple into his mouth, and fire burned straight down to her core. Her body clenched, so close to climax that she was blinded to anything but desire.

"Grady, oh God. Please. I need it."

He nipped her lightly, and she clung tighter than she ever had to anything. This was crazy. It wasn't sneaky, furtive, or risky, which had always added an extra something she needed. This was just pure animal desire. This was Grady.

He kissed his way up her chest, to her chin, finally to her mouth, and whispered against her lips. "Do you want it?"

"Yes. Please." She panted. "You know I do."

"I want to be inside you so bad my whole body aches." He punctuated his words with a roll of his hips that drove her mad.

"Then do it," she said on a moan of pleasure.

He fit his hand between them, cupped her, his palm sizzling hot against her damp panties. "Does that feel good?"

"Yes." She hiccupped with desire. "Please."

He was so gentle when she wanted and needed it

hard. Now. Right now.

"I want to touch you right here." He seduced her with his deep voice and the play of his palm against her, rotating, rubbing, heating her slowly to the boil. "I want to taste this." He stroked a finger straight along her center to the nub of her desire.

She could only moan his name.

"I could take you right here up against the door." He sank his teeth lightly into the soft flesh of her throat as his finger grazed all her heated parts. Then he licked where he'd bitten. "Or I could take you over there into the living room, lay you down on the carpet, spread your legs, and devour you with my mouth and my tongue."

She grabbed his ears, held on, her body rocking against his relentless touch. "Yes. All of it. Please, Grady."

"That's what I want," he whispered. "To taste every inch of you, to lick you until you scream, until you explode. Until you come into my mouth."

He seduced her with his words. She wanted everything. "Yes, yes, yes."

He moved fast, holding her tight in his arms, turning to take a few steps in the dark until he stood in a strip of moonlight falling through her living room window. Seamlessly, he let her feet slide to the floor before he swept them out from under her and had her flat on her back. He knelt between her legs while her skirt was up around her waist, her thighs bare and hot from his touch and the pinpoints of heat flaring in his eyes.

"You are so beautiful," he said from above her. He tore off his jacket, his tie, and popped a couple of buttons on his shirt. Then he braced himself with one arm as he flicked his finger along her center. "I can feel how wet you are even through your panties."

She couldn't joke. She couldn't beg. She couldn't even speak. All she could do was put her hand over his and show him what she craved.

"You don't want me to rush this."

She gasped as he drew his finger hard across her sensitive nub. "Yes, I do."

He slid beneath the side elastic and touched bare flesh for the first time. Hot, slick, wild bare flesh. Her whole body quivered as a rush of need flashed across her skin.

He played her length, dipping inside her, then swiping up the center again. "You're so wet for me. It makes me crazy how wet you are." He grabbed her hand and molded it to the front of his slacks. "Feel what you do to me."

He was a solid gold bar of flesh in her hand. She wanted him inside her. She loved hot, hard, and fast, as if that was a measure of how badly a man wanted her. But Grady wanted to taste her as much as he wanted to bury himself inside her.

"Taste me," she lured him. "Taste how wet I am for you. Taste how hard I come for you."

His eyes ablaze in the moonlight, he slipped his fingers beneath the waist of her panties and slid them down. Jordana pulled one leg up, and he left the lingerie to cling to her other thigh.

He dipped down to blow on her, and she shivered with how badly she needed his mouth. Coming down fully between her legs, he pulled apart the lips of her sex and taste-tested.

"God, baby, you are so good."

"Stop teasing," she whispered.

He didn't stop, taking her slowly, nibbling, licking, dipping his tongue into her center. He'd never needed lessons. Grady knew it all. She'd become the pupil as he taught her how damned good going slow could be.

She drew her legs higher, giving him everything, letting him take it all. She stretched her arms out, searching for the leg of the coffee table so she could hang on as she arched into him.

Finally, he cupped her butt and began his feast. Slow and steady, never letting up, licking her to the edge, but not quite allowing her to slip over. He circled and swirled and teased until her body was rocking to his rhythm. She gasped, moaned, squeezed her eyes shut, cried, begged.

He entered her with a finger, finding that special spot just around the corner. If he'd used a faster stroke, she could have maintained, but he was so damn slow, so damn perfect, so relentless. She was all heat and sensation, her skin flushed, her mind wild. Even her hands clutching the table leg started to ache with crushing need. When he added another finger, along with his tongue on her, her body began to shake. Her legs quaked. She heard someone wailing, and she knew the sound came out of her own mouth, her own wild need. Everything built, shot to her center, contracted, and exploded out. She cried his name, swore to God, shouted loud enough to bring her neighbors on the run, if they'd actually cared.

He went on and on, holding her down, his mouth fastened to her, fingers inside her. It was so good it hurt, and finally she had to crawl away just so she could breathe, or she would have died.

Grady followed, folding her into his arms, anchoring her with one leg over her thigh. His fingers played lazily along the crease of her butt. Her ears still rang with the aftermath of her climax, and her skin was sensitized to the caress of clothing against her.

How could his wife have left him? She was insane. Vanilla? Who cared when he could make a woman come like that? Grady was worth a thousand times whatever man she was cheating with. That was the problem with marriage and long-term relationships, people lost sight of how good they had it. They got tired. They abandoned you. And that was why Jordana loved those rosy first few weeks before boredom set in.

Fisting her fingers around the open lapels of his shirt, she snuggled closer, breathing in his sexy pheromone-laced scent. He pressed his hips against her, pulling her tight to his hard body.

"That only made me want you even more." His voice rumbled in his chest. "I want to sink inside you, feel you tighten around me, and fuck you right up to heaven."

She melted against him. There was nothing like a filthy word, especially from Grady, to send her into orbit. And he'd known it would. Because he'd watched that kiss in *Bridget Jones's Diary*. Watched, listened, and learned.

How could any woman lose her appreciation for this man?

Jordana had always known relationships ended, or at least most of the good parts of them did. For the first time, her belief in that wavered.

Grady made her wonder if she might have been wrong all along.

CHAPTER TWELVE

He'd always thought women liked pretty words, but Jordana was nothing like other women. She loved down and dirty, all out sexy, hot and risky. It was why she loved Bridget's kiss, because of that out-of-control word.

And with it, she rolled away from him, stood in one smooth move, straightened her shirt. Her panties still hung just above one knee, the wantonness of it so sexy to him that his heart did a slow roll in his chest.

Her taste filled his mouth, covered his lips, and her scent was all over him. He could still feel her shivers of pleasure as if they'd branded his skin. She'd climaxed with wild abandon, her body rolling even as he held her down to draw out every last ounce of sensation.

She made him feel alive. She made him feel like a man. She hadn't cried anyone's name but his when she came.

"Do me, Grady." She held out her hand. "I can't wait another minute. I'd do it right here if my condoms weren't in my bedroom."

144

He loved the unabashed admission, turning the practical into seductive. Then, as if she couldn't even wait to pull him to his feet, she dashed past the small dining table that separated the living room from the dim interior of the kitchen on the other side of a small bar. He followed her into the dark hallway. On the left was a bathroom and a small bedroom occupied by a desk and chair and a stationary bike that he could make out in the light falling through the window. She disappeared through a door to the right, and light suddenly spilled into the hall.

He couldn't say what he expected, but it wasn't the utter femininity of the room. Of course, she was feminine, but she was also neat and no-nonsense. But here, there were pinks and pastels, a bed covered with a thick, baby blue comforter, dust ruffle, and a profusion of pastel-colored pillows. A corner vanity was fronted by a ruffled curtain, each of the bedside tables also curtained beneath a small drawer. Pink lace covered the lampshades, bathing the room in a soft glow. More lacy curtains covered the window.

She stood at the end of the bed, her hair a sexy mess he itched to dig his fingers into. There had been something so damn hot about holding her still as he plundered her body. She hadn't quite smoothed the skirt, and it was still hiked up on one side. The panties he'd adored now lay in the middle of the carpet. Her blouse was skewed, the lace edge of her bra enticing him.

What would she want now? What would make her the hottest? He thought of James diving for Penelope, and Grady dove on Jordana. Picking her up high, he tossed her onto the bed, then crawled after her. Reaching past her, he pushed most of the pillows to the floor, leaving her laid out before him like a succulent dish.

"I want you naked now." He tore at her blouse and bra, freeing her beautiful breasts. Then he shoved her skirt up until she was bared to him. And he froze. "God, you are so beautiful." He ducked down and sucked the sweet cherry between her legs into his mouth.

"Oh my God." She cried out, arched, her body almost coming off the bed.

When he surfaced, his mouth wet from her, they both ripped at his shirt. Buttons flew, and the rasp of his zipper was as erotic as the rush of her breath. All he wanted was her naked flesh against his. One of his shoes cracked against the wall as she threw it, and he couldn't say what happened to the other.

And finally they were skin to skin. She was so damn hot, every inch of her igniting a fire in him.

"Inside me," she whispered.

He put his tongue in her mouth. It wasn't what she wanted, but it was what he craved. Her kiss, the taste of her mouth sweetened with the taste of her climax. He fell into that kiss, his body stretched out on top of hers, all that skin, all that heat.

She wriggled and her legs parted, his hips slipping between hers. He rubbed languorously against her. He could have entered her right then, but he loved her slippery folds. He loved her mouth, her skin. He didn't want to rush.

She mewled beneath him, and he raised his head. "Make me come again," she whispered against his lips. "I want to be coming when you enter me."

She knew what she wanted, what she needed, and his own excitement rose with hers. Her lack of inhibition fueled him.

"We need a condom." Her hand unfurled, and he realized she must have retrieved one from the side table or the vanity the second before he'd entered the room.

He rolled to the side, and she rolled with him, rising to straddle him. Not having used a condom in almost twenty years, he was afraid he might fumble. But Jordana took over, curling her warm hand around him.

She squeezed, and his body arched involuntarily. "My, my, Mr. Masterson, you do have the most gorgeous pleasure tool."

He laughed. "My pleasure tool?"

She smiled, sexy, wicked, seductive. "Yes. It's a tool, and it's all for my pleasure."

She made him want, made him laugh. And yes, he was here for her pleasure.

Leaning forward, she stroked him in the tight circle of her hand as she murmured, "You did this for me on the phone. It's so much better when it's my fingers wrapped around you, don't you think?"

He groaned. "God, yes."

"And it will be so much better when you're deep inside me."

He thrust hard into her fist. "Put it on. Now."

"Or you'll lose it just like this?" she teased.

"Yes," he admitted freely. She pushed him that close, with the weeks of teasing, her kisses, her scent always in his head.

"But you have to be really, really hard in order to put the condom on." She caressed his crown with her thumb.

His whole body wanted to shiver. "I'm as hard as a gun barrel ready to explode."

She laughed and leaned in for a quick but delicious kiss. "You do make me laugh."

He held her there, hovering over him. "And you make me want a whole lot of other things." Pushing her hand out of the way, he slid his fingers between her legs. "You're wet and you wanted to come again." He swiped his tongue along her mouth. "So get busy."

She had a gorgeous smile that never failed to set loose the trip wire in his chest with a burst of emotion he didn't want to analyze.

"Whatever you say." She rose slowly, ripped the condom open, and took him in hand, rolling it on at an excruciatingly slow pace. "There," she crooned. "All ready."

Grady wasted no time in grabbing her by the waist and rolling her beneath him again. "My turn." Falling between her spread legs, he teased her with the hard tip, caressing her moist flesh.

For one brief moment, he thought about all the things he'd missed because he'd been too complacent, too set in his routine. Jordana showed him how much more there could be and how much less he'd been willing to accept.

His gut tightened as she squirmed beneath him. She gripped his arms, her fingers digging in. "I'm pretty sure I didn't teach you all this stuff."

"I'm improvising. Isn't that what a good pupil does?"

"Oh you're good, all right." She gasped and arched, as if he'd found a different and particularly sensitive spot. Then she growled. "Ooh, yes. You do this as well as you kiss." She furrowed her fingers up and down his arms.

"How many gold stars?"

"Billions and billions."

Then he used his fingers on her. Her skin was flushed, her folds wet with desire, but he wanted her on the edge, just starting to fall when he entered her. The way she said she wanted it, too. "Is this even better?"

She bit her lip, her eyes closing. Then she opened her mouth slightly for a gasp of breath. "Grady, yes, just like that."

He circled and caressed, dipped inside her, then back out, using his fingers to tease her the way he'd used his tongue on her earlier.

Her forehead scrunched in concentration, and her eyes squeezed tightly shut. He loved watching her in the pink light of the lace over her lamps. Her skin was flushed, her nipples pearled. When she threw her arms over her head and braced herself on the headboard, pushing back on him, he knew she was close, so damn close. His heart was beating three times its limit when he felt her body start to quake.

He took her then, plunging deep into her. Jesus, it was better than anything. She held him tight, her body clamped hard around him, moving, undulating, and it literally drove him mad. He wanted to pound hard, fast, ride her right down into the mattress. But with his one last ounce of control, he pulled back slightly, and short-stroked inside her, right on that delicious spot he'd discovered with his fingers.

Jordana went wild then, crying out his name. Her legs up high around his hips, she grabbed his backside and pulled him in tight. "Harder, oh God, yes, please, harder, Grady. Hard, hard, hard."

He gave her what she wanted and what he needed,

slammed into her. It was heaven. He closed his eyes and strained deeper into her, the tight fit of her body around him glorious.

And then she did something amazing, fitting her hand between them, God only knew how, her fingers finding the base of his sex. She pressed, squeezed, molded, and he exploded from the inside out, shouting, groaning, coming hard, forever and ever.

He came to his senses sometime later, their arms, legs, and bodies tangled. It was impossible to move. Every limb had turned boneless. He was fused inside her, feeling a few remaining tremors like aftershocks of the big one. Occasionally her body undulated around him, tightened, relaxed. Their sex was redolent in the air, tangy and salty.

He rubbed his nose in her hair, the sweet fragrance of citrus teasing his nose. The spice of her first orgasm still lingered in his mouth.

"A billion gold stars for that one," she whispered.

"You deserve quite a few gold stars yourself."

She shifted slightly and he realized he was crushing her into the bed, but when he started to move, she clung to him. "Don't go yet."

He hadn't intended to leave, but her words reminded him this wasn't a normal relationship. He wouldn't be spending the night, wouldn't make love to her again in the dark, wouldn't wake up beside her in the morning.

The lightness of air around them suddenly seemed heavier, but all he said was, "I'm not leaving yet. I just didn't want to crush you."

She snuggled deeper. "I like your weight on me." Then he felt her laugh against his shoulder. "I can't believe you told her we were serial killers."

For a moment, he had no idea what she was talking about. Then he remembered the girl. "I was just trying to warn her of the dangers of picking up strangers in bars."

She laughed again.

"But I have to admit I enjoyed her attitude. She was like you, not afraid of anything."

She shook her head slightly. "I'm afraid of stuff."

"I meant sexually. I like how uninhibited you are." He tapped the tip of her nose. "I especially liked that thing you did to me at the end."

"Sent you over the edge, huh?"

"Yeah." He didn't ask who had taught her that, the foreman or the man who put her cold hand between his warm thighs or the engineer who took her up against the shower wall. Grady probably wouldn't have had the nerve to do any of those things.

But he wanted to have the nerve now. With her. "Teach me everything you know."

She snorted lightly. "That's a tall order. I'm a slut, after all."

He held her face. "Don't talk yourself down."

Her blue eyes were suddenly bright. "I wasn't."

"You were. But I like how much you love sex. It makes it hotter when you take charge or you do something unexpected like that little trick to make me explode."

She untangled one arm to put her hand to his cheek. "The word *slut* doesn't bother me. And I'm glad you like my lack of inhibition. I'll have to think up some really naughty stuff for you." Then she squirmed. "But now I have to use the bathroom."

He felt something spiral down inside him. It was over. "I should do that, too." He had to get rid of the condom.

"There's another bathroom in the hall."

He'd seen it, and, as hard as it was to do, he pulled out and climbed off the bed. Jordana slid off the other side.

Her hair was a mess, her mascara smudged, her lipstick gone, but with all her luscious curves, she was the most beautiful creature he'd ever seen.

She disappeared into her bathroom, and he grabbed his clothes off the carpet and headed out to the hall bathroom he'd seen.

After he'd dressed, he returned to her bedroom to find she'd pulled a robe on and combed her hair.

"I kind of like the just-had-sex hair," he told her.

She smiled. "Oh my, Mr. Masterson, you are getting racy."

"It was a badge of honor that I was able to do that to you." He shouldered into his jacket. He didn't know what to do now. Kiss her goodnight? Beg her to let him stay? Change the rules of their lessons? This couldn't be called a relationship. They weren't even supposed to have sex. It was supposed to be all talk and no action. But things had gotten all turned around.

Now he didn't want to leave her. He wanted to sleep with her in his arms. He wanted… God, he just wanted.

But he still had a wife, and he couldn't think about a future while he still had a past and a present that included Darlene, even if she had dumped him.

Jordana didn't want him to leave, but she hadn't a clue how to ask him to stay. He hadn't kissed her goodnight or anything normal couples would do. But they weren't normal and this wasn't a relationship so she couldn't expect that.

He liked her lack of inhibition. He loved her stories. He thought she was sexy, and he wanted to learn all her naughty tricks. And God, could that man hit all her special hot spots, giving her more pleasure than anyone ever had. Maybe more than she'd ever allowed herself with all the quickies she'd thought she adored.

The echo of the door closing behind him still filled her suddenly tiny apartment. She didn't bother to turn on the lights, but flopped down on the couch and lay in the dark. She could see the stars through the open living room window.

A billion stars.

Grady made her see stars. He made her laugh. He made her feel good about herself. He made her climax so hard she wailed. It was a new experience, letting herself go like that. She was so used to furtive, sexy, risky couplings that she'd learned how to hit the peak very quietly. Somehow it was so much better when she was loud. But no man had made her scream like Grady did. She'd dallied with her last friend with benefits at his apartment, and he'd been too worried about the neighbors to make much noise. But then Jordana had never needed to scream like she did for Grady.

He was teaching her about new things she wanted, like having sex on a comfy bed, screaming out how good it felt, laying for a while in his arms afterward instead of rushing to fumble their clothes back on. Maybe even having breakfast together in the morning.

Those long minutes in his arms had been so darn good, the best she'd ever felt. She wanted more.

But Grady wasn't the friends-with-benefits type. And he was married. Bringing him home with her had probably been far more risky than letting her engineer take her in the ladies' room.

CHAPTER THIRTEEN

Sunday dinner at his mother's was served early, at three in the afternoon. Mom claimed it gave the body several hours to digest a big meal before having to go to bed.

And Mom cooked big. This time it was roast beef and Yorkshire pudding, a British recipe she'd gotten years ago from a dear friend.

His big family was seated around the dining table in the formal dining room with all the best china and silver. His mother insisted on using the best rather than letting it sit in the sideboard only to come out twice a year at Christmas and Thanksgiving.

Mom still lived in the same house in Saratoga that Grady had grown up in, which meant there were six bedrooms to maintain. But she was an adorable creature of habit who'd lived with the same traditions all her married life, and she wouldn't leave this house until they carried her out. And she needed the big house, too, with four sons, Grady, Trent, Alec, and Nate in that birth order, one

155

daughter, Chelsea, the youngest, a daughter-in-law, son-in-law, and six grandchildren. The dining room with its high ceiling was a riot of noise at the opposite end of the table where the grandchildren, all under the age of ten, and their respective parents were seated.

"Please pass the gravy." Grady nudged his brother Trent, who was a slightly younger but unmarried version of himself, even down to his belief in how Yorkshire pudding should be demolished. Hence the fact that the gravy boat was almost empty. A Yorkshire wasn't pudding at all, but more like a popover. They rose in the oven until a hole appeared in the center and the object was to fill it with as much gravy as possible. And that's exactly what Grady did.

Seated on his left at the head of the table, his mother tapped his arm. "Dear, you should really talk Darlene out of working on Sunday. It can't be good for her digestion." Mom, bless her heart, was all about the digestion. People with good digestion lived longer.

"Darlene doesn't listen to anything he says," Chelsea offered, although how she could have heard the conversation over the cacophony at her end of the table, he didn't have a clue. Maybe it had something to do with being a mother of three. His baby sister, her long, dark hair piled prettily in a knot on top of her head, had never gotten on well with Darlene.

Even his sister was unwittingly helping him make the lie bigger and better.

Maybe he should have started off telling the truth. He hadn't wanted to come at all. Contemplating hot sex with Jordana was much better than telling his family that his wife had left him, then answering the limitless questions.

Jordana. She was so much easier to be with. Not only was making love to her as hot as stepping into lava, it was fun. It wasn't, however, guilt free. If he told his family about Darlene, then he'd have to think about the guilty part of being with Jordana. And he didn't want to deal with any of that.

Actually he didn't want to think at all. He'd rather show up on Jordana's doorstep, muscle her into her apartment when she opened the door, and do all the dirty, naughty, sexy things he wanted. And Jordana would let him. Last night he'd sent her a text saying that he couldn't stop thinking of her sweet taste. She'd sent him back a devil-face emoticon.

This was all so damn crazy.

He was married, and instead of handling the divorce, he was fooling around with a younger woman.

He'd been comfortable with his life, even if he couldn't say he'd been ecstatically happy. Now he'd fallen into a relationship that was just as easy. It had simply happened. He hadn't needed to do a thing.

He was good at his job, but in his personal life, he was… complacent. There had to be something wrong with that. He still wore his wedding ring, too, so he didn't have to explain anything to anyone, not his family, not at work.

"Mom, you do not need to get the gravy," Nate said over the din at his end of the table. Three of the six grandchildren were his. "Grady finished it. Let him refill it."

Anyone would have thought Nate was the eldest the way he directed everyone, and maybe that was because he was a polished, confident attorney who always dealt with the rule of law. And the law was that Mom shouldn't have to do everything, especially after she'd spent all day cooking.

Grady had been daydreaming and missed the beginning of the argument. "I'll get it." He grabbed the gravy boat and headed to the kitchen.

He was amazed by his family. As many of them as there were, they all made time for Sunday. They made time for their mother.

The only one who hadn't, he realized, was Darlene. Sometimes she'd claimed a migraine or too much work, or whatever, and she'd sent him alone, an occurrence that had become more frequent over the last few months.

Had she been meeting Mr. GQ on those Sundays she'd missed?

He accidentally sloshed gravy onto the stove instead of into the boat.

"Honey, what's bothering you?"

He hadn't even heard his mother enter. "What? Nothing. Just made a mistake," he lied. Another lie.

She grabbed a sponge and wiped up the mess he'd made on her ceramic cooktop. Last summer, he and his brothers had taken a week off work and put in a new kitchen for her. Their father had taught them to be handy with tools, and the old kitchen had been the original from the seventies.

"Are you and Darlene having problems?"

Her question punched him right in the center of his chest. It was darn near a knock-out blow.

All his other stories could be construed as lies of omission. Or excuses. But anything he said now to put his mother off the scent would be an out-and-out lie that could come back to haunt him.

And really, why didn't he tell the truth? The answer was pathetic. Once he told his mother the truth, he'd be forced to do something about it.

There was truly something wrong with a man who couldn't face up to reality.

"She's divorcing me." There, it was out. And strangely, he didn't feel so bad now that it was said.

Words seemed to fail his mother for several seconds. "Why didn't you tell me you two were having trouble?"

"Because we weren't. At least I was totally oblivious to it." The gravy boat filled, he set it on the counter and turned to lean back, crossing his arms. "I thought we were fine. Obviously we weren't."

"But—"

"Grady, where's the gravy?" Nate shouted from the dining room. "My Yorkshire's getting cold."

"Nate, come and get it yourself," his mother called, her tone sharper than usual.

Nate stomped into the kitchen. While Trent and Alec were physically more like Grady, Nate was stocky with light brown hair which was starting to thin even though he was only thirty-six "What are you two doing?" He had very keen senses, and Grady cursed him for it.

"None of your bee's wax," their mother said. "Take the gravy." She handed him the boat.

"But everything's getting cold," Nate said, his eyes wide with amazement. Mom loved her food hot.

She made an eye roll at him. "We're busy."

He backed out, totally nonplussed.

"We can talk about it later, Mom," Grady said. "Another day, without the whole family listening in on all the details. Let's eat."

"Grady, I'm here for you, honey."

He pulled her in for a quick hug. "I know. But this is new for me, too. And Darlene hasn't said a whole lot about why." Except that he was vanilla in the bedroom and she was having an affair with a sexy younger stud from the office. "She and I need to talk more, but I'm letting her settle herself first."

"She'll come to her senses."

"Maybe she already has, Mom." Maybe Darlene was bringing him to his senses, too.

There was more than what they'd had in their marriage. He'd asked Jordana to teach him what women wanted, but she'd also shown him that he'd let routine and complacency rule his life. She'd brought freshness into his world. She made him feel alive. She'd woken him up.

He didn't want to go back to sleep again.

Mom put her hand on his arm. "This will be our little secret, and we'll talk when you're ready."

There was nothing more to talk about.

The coffee in the pot had been sitting too long, its stewed scent permeating the conference room. They'd reached the eighth item on the agenda for the Monday morning staff meeting, after all the VPs' reports.

Presiding over his staff of eight vice presidents, Brett Baker sat at the head of the ten-seat oak conference table, the sun streaming in through the window behind him. He held the paper closer as if he needed reading glasses, despite the fact that even at the age of fifty, their CEO still had the eyesight of an eagle. "You want Jordana to have Andrew's old office?"

"What?" Rhonda chirped loudly. She grabbed her glasses off the table and stuffed them on her nose. The item was clearly news to her.

Grady had to smile. Jordana was ingenious. He'd overheard part of the discussion about the office, and Rhonda was her usual negative self. Despite what she'd said, she never would have brought it up in the meeting.

"Well," Rhonda finally said. "She and I have discussed it, but…"

"I believe it's essential," Gloria said right over her. Gloria King was an efficient, no-nonsense CEO who'd worked for them a little less than a year. Grady respected her opinions. So did the rest of the staff.

"What's the issue?" Brett wanted to know.

Without letting Rhonda speak, Gloria said, "My issue is the confidential nature of everything Jordana does. My payroll clerk has an office. Jordana needs one, too."

"All the employee files are in my office," Rhonda protested.

Gloria lifted a hand off the arm of her chair, her index finger pointed. "But her computer is out in the open."

Grady debated keeping his mouth shut. If he added too much to the debate, Rhonda might start to wonder why he cared. Yet he couldn't sit still without lending his support to what Gloria was saying. "The office is empty. And Gloria's correct, Rhonda. There's too much risk having her in a cubicle where her work is accessible to anyone."

"But I need my admin within easy reach." Rhonda

stopped short of actually whining.

Seated next to Rhonda, and opposite Grady, Court Stevens turned his gaze heavenward. As VP of Manufacturing, his group was the largest, and therefore he had the most contact with Rhonda regarding employee issues. He'd also had his fair share of run-ins with her.

As for Grady, he'd worked across from Rhonda for a year and a half. She had her expertise, but she didn't like detail. She left all that to her admin, which was probably why her previous assistant had quit. Jordana had taken any project Rhonda threw at her and excelled in every detail. But Rhonda wanted to keep her under her thumb. Jordana was too good for that.

Brett stroked his chin. "I wonder if you actually need a new admin as well, so that Jordana can concentrate on employee relations. We're going to need an HR manager. Why not choose her? You just told us in your report that we'll be increasing staff at least twenty percent by the end of the year."

Grady considered this a very sensible argument.

Gloria's mouth twitched in a smile while Rhonda sputtered. "That's ridiculous. You can't have a VP, a manager, and an admin as the only employees in one department."

"HR is a function, not a department, Rhonda." Knox Turner, VP of Engineering, just had to get his dig in. Rhonda had resented him from that moment one year ago when he'd refused to support her bid to become a VP.

She practically growled at Knox. Being a function and not a department had been her argument for taking the department out of Accounting and Administration and appointing her the VP of a *function* with only two employees. She didn't like Knox throwing it back at her now.

Lucy Perez added her two cents. As VP of Management Information Systems, she had extensive contact with Jordana for any computer or communications issues that came up. "You and Jordana alone aren't going to be able to keep up with the demand. And when we go public…" She spread her hands, not even needing to finish the sentence.

"I agree, Rhonda. You can't keep up without adding headcount." Brett stared her down when she started to protest again. "Figure out an appropriate salary adjustment and get it done."

"If we're going to do this, shouldn't we at least interview outside?" Rhonda sniffed primly, like a snooty old woman. "After all, Jordana's only been here nine months. Not even a year."

Grady wanted to smack her, metaphorically speaking, but before he could say how ridiculous the idea was, Brett shook his head. "She's doing a great job, and our policy is to promote from within wherever possible."

There wasn't another protest to make, and Rhonda wisely shut her mouth, letting Brett move along with the agenda.

Grady didn't, however, miss the way Rhonda's pen gouged the paper as she made notes.

Jordana would get the promotion and the office, but Rhonda would find a way to make her pay.

"Lunch," Gloria hissed as she passed her cubicle.

"When?" Jordana was restless after a morning of never-ending employee chatter. That had been a good thing, though, because it put a stop to her replaying Friday night with Grady over and over in her head. There'd been one text and that was all. They'd had this weird tacit agreement not to call each other, as if they'd both needed to consider the line they'd crossed. Not just a line, a barbed wire border between countries, even a whole new frontier.

"Now," Gloria insisted, yanking Jordana back to the present. "Get your things and meet me out front."

Fifteen minutes later, they were seated on the patio of their favorite Mexican restaurant. Gloria had kept her mouth shut during the entire drive even though she was obviously bursting to tell. "You are not going to believe this," she said. She was highly animated, which was unusual for Gloria.

"What?"

"Brett has decided to make you HR Manager."

Jordana's mouth dropped open.

"But I got you the office." Gloria buffed her pretty rose-colored nails on her jacket sleeve. "Okay," she added, "I admit Grady Masterson helped on that, too. We both put in a word for you."

Jordana was utterly speechless. Grady and Gloria had achieved success on the office and the CEO had promoted her to manager? It was too much to take in. The place was a babble of voices and salsa music played just a little too loud. Out on the road, cars whooshed by and the low wall between them and the sidewalk did nothing to stem the flow of exhaust fumes. They should have eaten inside. She couldn't think out here.

"You were a genius for getting the office on the agenda, you sneaky girl." Gloria put up a hand for a high five. She was far more excited than Jordana had ever seen her.

Jordana herself was feeling a little giddy. "I didn't sneak it on there." She *tsk*ed. "Well, it was a partial sneak. Rhonda said she'd bring it up at the staff meeting." She shrugged. "But I knew she wouldn't."

The waiter brought their taco salads, and Gloria tucked into hers. "She wouldn't have. She was totally shocked seeing it on the agenda." She leaned forward. "I'm really proud of you for standing up for yourself."

Jordana put a hand over her mouth, trying to hide her goofy smile. "But what's this manager thing?"

"Once I went to bat for you about the office, Grady joined in. Then Brett said you should be a manager, so you'd have the authority an admin wouldn't." Gloria smiled. "I tell you, all the other VPs were right on it, too. Make it happen," she said, dropping into an imitation of Brett's deep tone.

"Thank you, Gloria. You're the best." Jordana put her hands to her burning cheeks. Everyone had gone to bat for her. Gloria. Brett. Grady. Thank God Grady hadn't been the one to bring up the promotion or Rhonda would wondered if something was going on. They didn't need that scrutiny because Rhonda was going to watch her every move now. Technically, she should inform Rhonda and the company about their relationship. But they didn't *have* a relationship. She didn't know exactly what they did have, but it wasn't a *relationship*. So for the time being, *technically* didn't apply. At least that's what she told herself.

But there were other concerns, too. Jordana made a face. "This isn't going to be as good as you think."

"Why not?"

Jordana shook her head. "It might have been better if I'd talked Rhonda around to it eventually. She could make my life miserable over this."

Gloria leaned one elbow on the table. "Then why did you put the office on the agenda?"

"That was just the office. She said she'd discuss it, and if she called me on it, I could throw that back in her face and tell her I thought that's what she wanted. Since that's what she *said*. But the office *and* manager?" She clenched her teeth. "I don't know. This could be a disaster."

Gloria put her fork down. "Do not make a catastrophe out of this before you even start." She held up her hands, fingers splayed, in a definite stop-the-madness motion. "Just show Rhonda how good you are at your job."

Gloria didn't know Rhonda well enough. And neither did Grady if he actually thought there wouldn't be a fallout.

"Here's what you need to take stock of." Gloria held up a finger. "You've got four VPs who spoke up for you." She held up another finger. "And even better, you've got Brett in your corner. He said you're doing a great job."

"Wow." That was awesome. And Gloria was right. She sounded like a pessimist. She'd handle Rhonda. She always had. "I really appreciate you sticking up for me."

"Of course. It was the least I could do since I pushed you into taking Andrew's office."

Jordana flapped her hand dismissively. "You didn't

push. I knew it had to be done." Then she changed the subject. "So tell me about the interview last week with Parker Hunt. I read your notes, and Brett's reviewing what all the other VPs had to say, but how did it really go?"

Gloria quickly grabbed up her fork again as if she were starving. "It was fine. I asked him if he thought we could work together without any issues, and he said yes."

"Everyone else thought he'd be a great fit, too."

Compared to her former animation, Gloria was now slightly subdued. "He's good at what he does. And he was always easy to work with. Everyone should get along with him." She managed a wry smile. "Even Rhonda."

"So you're okay with everything?"

"Completely." She looked directly at Jordana. Maybe too directly. "We're both adults and can keep the past in the past. And I've told Brett that we worked together. Not about—" She shrugged so she didn't have to actually say they'd dated. "But I wanted him to be aware."

"Good. That's great." That they'd been at the same company at the same time would eventually come out anyway. And when it did, Brett would wonder why Gloria hadn't mentioned it. "And for the record, Parker charmed Rhonda, too."

"Yes." Gloria nodded, her gaze on her plate and her mind on something deep inside. "He's quite charming."

There was a story there, Jordana was sure. But she couldn't ask when Gloria was so obviously not offering.

Of course, the mention of Rhonda brought the promotion back to mind. And that made her think of Grady, too. She needed to thank him for sticking up for her.

But first she'd have to deal with Rhonda.

There was no choice but a direct confrontation. Jordana didn't even go around to her desk first. She marched right up to Rhonda's second entrance, the one which faced Jordana's new office.

Rhonda was seated at her desk, a folder in front of her. She wasn't writing, and since she didn't have her glasses on, Jordana wasn't even sure she was reading. She was just sitting there.

Jordana knocked lightly and stepped inside. The opposite door was open as well, with a view across her cubicle and into Grady's office. He looked up, their eyes met, and suddenly it was Friday night again on the living room floor of her apartment with Grady in the moonlight, Grady between her legs, Grady doing all those luscious things to her.

Her skin was suddenly flushed, her breath fast, and her blood rushed through her ears.

"Well, you pulled off that little coup quite nicely."

She snapped back to Rhonda. She couldn't afford even the slightest distraction or Rhonda would pounce. "It wasn't a coup. You and I talked about it on Thursday."

Rhonda swiveled in her chair, then crossed her legs, pulling her skirt down to the knee. She wore only knee-length skirts or dresses. Jordana wondered what Rhonda's husband was like. He'd never been to any of the company parties. Maybe he didn't actually exist.

"I've had a good think about it." Rhonda picked up a pen, flipping it back and forth between her fingers. "And

I've come to the conclusion that Brett has a point."

Jordana didn't allow herself the proverbial jaw drop, but she did feel her eyes bug slightly. "He has a point? What does that mean?" There had to be a catch.

"With the new staffing levels once we start shipping product, I can't handle the workload on my own."

Rhonda couldn't handle it? Jordana was the one who'd have the increased workload since she dealt with the employees. "It's going to be a lot more work for both of us," Jordana said diplomatically.

"So I agree with him that we need a manager with the appropriate authority level." Rhonda keep flipping that pen in her fingers, giving it an inordinate amount of attention rather than looking at Jordana. "I'm just not sure about your level of experience."

Jordana clamped her teeth tight. Then she swallowed. The clench hurt a little, but it forced her to think before she jumped on Rhonda and started screaming. "I've got quite a lot of experience, as you will recall. And since coming here, I've had my hand in just about every HR task that's arisen."

Rhonda jerked her head up. Jordana was sure she heard her neck cracking. "What about the ones that haven't arisen?" Rhonda demanded.

"Like what?"

"Sexual harassment. Discrimination. Have you ever fired an employee?"

Rhonda knew she hadn't. All Jordana had done was handle the paperwork for the two employees that had been fired during her tenure at the company. But Rhonda hadn't fired them either. Their individual bosses had done that.

"I'm sure those are things I can consult with you on.

You'd have to be involved anyway." Firing, harassment, or discrimination would be handled at the highest level, especially if there might be the danger of a lawsuit.

"There will be a lot of things I can't delegate." Rhonda pursed her lips ever so matronly and primly.

Jordana had the strongest urge to ask why Rhonda had chosen the human relations field. She didn't even like people.

It was time to stop fighting and explaining and making counterarguments. "I can do this, Rhonda. I'll be good at it. I'll appreciate any help you can give me, all your advice." She wasn't brownnosing. Rhonda understood all the rules and regulations and she knew how just about every situation should be handled, even if her people skills sucked. That's what she needed Jordana for. Jordana had the people skills. "If you give me a chance, we can make a good team."

Rhonda was quiet so long that Jordana prepared herself for the next slam. It didn't come. Which was almost as jaw-dropping as the fact that Rhonda had agreed with Brett's point.

"You've got your office." Rhonda threw her pen on the desk, where it rolled until it fell over the other edge. "And you've got your promotion."

Jordana wasn't naturally speechless. She talked for a living. But Rhonda had stunned her.

"Aren't you going to say thank you?"

"Thank you." Then Jordana went for it. "I'll start moving my things over to the new office." She'd also need to call MIS to have her computer transferred. The computer techs would freak if she unplugged it herself. They'd handle the phones, too. "Do you want me to get the file cabinets out of here as well?" She could have someone from Facilities move them.

Rhonda snorted with disgust. "Of course. I'm tired of having you traipse in here all the time. Besides, isn't that why you said you needed the office?"

Jordana didn't rise to Rhonda's baiting. She'd gotten what she wanted, and now she could be magnanimous. "Great. I'll take care of everything." She always did.

Flapping her hand, Rhonda shooed her out of the office.

There might still be a big catch. Maybe Rhonda would only give her a dollar raise or something equally ridiculous. But Jordana had attained her goal a lot sooner than she'd ever hoped for.

When she left by the opposite door, Grady was watching her, his expression a solid mask of nothing. Until she winked at him.

Along with Gloria and Brett, Grady deserved a big thank you.

But she was a manager now. She couldn't send him a sext. She couldn't call during work hours. She had to be on her best behavior.

Until *after* office hours.

CHAPTER FOURTEEN

Grady tried not to watch her, but whenever he passed Jordana's desk or she left her cubicle, some internal radar went up. His senses were working overtime, and even though the weekend had passed, he could still taste her, feel her fingers on him, smell the sweet tang of her citrus scent on the air.

She returned from lunch and immediately entered Rhonda's office. He could see her the whole time. There hadn't been a lot of shouting. Not a single object flew across the room. Jordana even winked at him as she walked into her cubicle when the big showdown was over.

Picking up his phone, he sent her a text. *What happened?*

She shot back a reply. *I can't sext anymore. I'm a manager.* She added a few happy face emoticons.

He didn't smile. Rhonda might see him. *That wasn't sexting. I didn't say anything dirty.* But his heart was thumping just the same. *Meet me later. I still need my lessons.*

Her reply was stern. *No more texting until after office*

hours!!!!!!! She added a devil face.

He still didn't smile, but it was killing him to hide it.

He kept on watching her throughout the afternoon. She gathered boxes and packed up all her binders, office supplies, files, and the various things women kept in their drawers. Nina from MIS arrived to transfer her computer. Ivy stood on her tiptoes to look over the divider. "You can't leave me alone between the two of them," he heard her hiss.

Was he that bad?

No. He was becoming very, very good. At least as far as Jordana was concerned.

He waited until after five o'clock. He waited for Ivy to leave and for Rhonda to pick up her briefcase and lock her office doors. He waited until the chatter of keyboards was silenced. Then he waited a little longer.

Closing up, he headed past the empty warren of cubicles, past Rhonda's second door, turned the corner. Jordana's new office was the only door still open.

He felt a lightness in his bones as he headed her way. Darlene had ceased to exist. His guilt was stuffed deep down inside. For now, there was only Jordana and all the things he wanted from her.

When he stopped in her doorway, she was typing on her cell phone. "Thanks for putting in a good word for me with Brett. I appreciate that." She was still typing.

"You're welcome. Mostly it was Gloria. She really believes in you."

His phone beeped with a text. "Excuse me a second." He read what she'd sent him, and his skin turned to fire.

You need to earn another gold star. What are you going to do to deserve it?

His blood headed south, and his pants were suddenly too tight.

"Thanks again," she said brightly. "I'll see you tomorrow."

"Have a good evening." He backed away. The game was entertaining.

"You, too."

He started typing the moment he couldn't see her anymore.

We're going for a drive. Take off your panties.

Jordana's heart was a hard, fast thudding in her chest. She was wet the second she read the word *panties*.

While she was in the ladies' room, he texted her again. *If the bra isn't a front clasp, take that off, too.*

Her lingerie happened to be lacy with a front hook. She left it on, but stuffed her panties in her purse.

She was crazy. She'd just been promoted to HR Manager, and she was fooling around with the VP of Business Development. But she couldn't let it end. She was a desire junkie after all. And she was jonesing for Grady.

She was skipping down the stairs when his next text came in. *Drive to the Costco parking lot. I'll meet you there.*

A door closed on the landing above. "Jordana, hold up." The CEO's voice.

She almost tripped on a step.

Brett jogged down to her, briefcase in hand. He was an extremely well-preserved fifty, a big man at well over six

174

feet, but all muscle, no flab. His thick blond hair was white at the temples, and he had the lines around his eyes of a man who got his exercise out of doors. She'd always found him impressive, maybe even a little scary.

Especially when she wasn't wearing panties.

"I wanted to say congratulations on your promotion."

She stuffed away any thought of Grady and her panties—or lack thereof. "I understand I have you to thank for that."

"Thank yourself. You've been doing an excellent job. You were overqualified as an admin when we hired you, and you're certainly proven you can handle the new position."

Now this was a boss to emulate. Rhonda could use a few lessons from him. Thank goodness Jordana, rather than Rhonda, was the one who gave the seminars on how to prepare employee reviews.

"Thank you." She actually felt herself glow under his praise.

He clapped her on the upper arm. "You probably won't be thanking us when we really ramp up the staffing."

Jordana continued down the stairs beside him. "I'm prepared. By the way, I sent my recommendation to Rhonda on the new Marketing VP."

He nodded. Even with her high heels, he made her feel short. She liked tall men. She loved the fact that Grady made her feel so small and delicate.

Oops. No thinking about Grady right now.

"Everyone seems to approve of Parker Hunt," Brett observed.

"That's the consensus."

"Draft up the offer letter tomorrow then, and I'll sign

it."

"Will do."

He opened the outside door for her. "Parking lot's empty." He poked a finger at her. "You work too late. I almost always see your car out here when I'm leaving. And Grady's."

A chill skittered along her spine like an insect. Brett was noticing a little too much. "There's always so much to do."

He headed to his big cream-colored luxury model, adding before he'd gone too far, "Better get busy finding your replacement admin."

"My replacement?" She sounded a little dumb.

"You've got more important things to do, Jordana." Then he waved. "Have a good night."

Rhonda hadn't said anything about a replacement. Honestly, she thought she'd be doing both jobs, just like always. It had seemed enough of a concession just to get the office and the new title. If she'd worried about Rhonda's reprisals before, she really better be on the look-out now since the HR payroll budget was going to be shot for the year.

She'd have to be very careful with Grady. Rhonda would be watching her like a hawk circling over the hapless bunny who'd suddenly broken out into the open.

But she wasn't giving him up. She was too hooked on the high he gave her. She wanted whatever he had planned for her tonight. But no more sexting during the day, no more meets at Leo's or role-plays in bars on University Avenue. As long as they kept everything after office hours and out of local hang-outs, they should be safe.

She found him pacing beside his car at the far end of

the Costco lot where the only open spaces were left.

"Sorry. Brett stopped me."

He just stared at her, his eyes dark with heat, as if he'd been thinking about what he was going to do to her. "Follow me," he finally said.

"Where are we going?"

"You'll find out."

The mystery excited her as much as his intensity. His gaze traveled her body. "Did you do what I asked?"

He was making her wet. She had the shivers of a sexual high. "I'm not wearing panties."

"Even when you were with Brett?" His voice got deeper, heavier.

"He caught me just after I took them off."

He stepped into her quickly, crowding her up against the car without actually touching her. "You make me crazy," he whispered.

He couldn't possibly understand what he did to her.

"And the bra?" he asked softly, looking down the front of her shirt.

"It undoes in the front."

"Good." His voice was as soft as butterfly wings across her cheek.

She wanted to grab him by the suit jacket and pull his mouth down to hers. But they were already taking a risk standing so close together.

As if he suddenly had the same thought, he backed off. "Now get in your car and follow me."

"Yes, sir." She saluted.

For the first time, he smiled, a wicked grin that promised a retribution she was going to love.

His heart was an erratic thump by the time he reached the county park tucked away against the foothills of the Santa Cruz Mountains. It lay along a back road through a wooded area that eventually let out onto Highway 9, which would lead up to the summit at Skyline and down the other side into Santa Cruz. He'd sometimes come out here for a hike and had seen practically no one. Darlene had never been a hiker.

He turned into a small dirt clearing that served as a parking lot and backed in, the car's nose facing out so that he could see if anyone else happened along. The road was barely visible through a thicket of trees, and no one would see them in here.

Jordana pulled in beside him and rolled down her window.

"Get in my backseat," he told her. He liked giving orders. He liked it even better when Jordana followed them.

In mere seconds, she'd opened the back door. Once she was inside, Grady rolled down the front windows halfway to give them air, then got out and joined her in the backseat of the car.

He crooked his finger at her, and she leaned close, her lips parted. His body was heavy and hard. He had condoms in his pocket, which he'd purchased over the weekend. But right now, he wanted her mouth.

"Kiss me," he demanded.

"I didn't teach you that," she said, her lips far too many inches from his.

"Teach me what?" He let her scent cloud his mind, his gaze on her mouth, on those sweet lips.

"To order me around."

"Do you like it?" They breathed the same air. It was so damn sexy to be this close and not touch her. Like he was a little boy waiting until no one noticed before he stole the last cookie on the plate. Jordana was the treat he craved.

"I like it very much."

Need exploded in his chest. "Then freaking kiss me when I tell you to." He shoved his hand up under her hair, cupped her nape and pulled her in tight, only an inch separating their bodies. "Do it now."

"Yes, Mr. Masterson." She dove on him then, pushing his head back against the seat, her body plastered to his, her breasts flattened against his chest.

She kissed him with her whole body, her lips taking his, her tongue invading his mouth, her arms heating him, her tight nipples scoring his skin, her hair a silky curtain around them. She stole his breath. She stole his mind.

Their breath came as fast as race horses, their hearts pounding against each other like hoof beats. She pulled back. "Was that good enough?"

"More."

She dove into him again. Her mouth locked on his, she cupped his hands to her breasts. He fumbled open three buttons until he touched lace.

Her body twisted against him, and she angled her head to take his lips again. She kissed, licked, nipped, sucked. Then she whispered, "Don't stop now."

He flicked the clasp, and her gorgeous breasts spilled into his hands. He pinched each nipple, and she growled her pleasure deep in her throat.

Steam rose off his skin. His body was hard enough to drive deep into her with a single thrust. And she was naked under that skirt.

"Get on top of me now." The command's effect was lost in the hoarse groan of his voice.

But Jordana had obviously been dying for the demand. Straddling his lap, the skirt rode high, and then her arms enveloped him again, her hair fell around them, her mouth feasted on him. The musky sweet scent of her arousal filled his head. He was nothing now but a machine without thought, with only the need to take. With her nipple between his fingers, molding her, teasing her, he dropped a hand between her legs.

Jesus, she was wet. She moaned as his fingers slipped along her center. He played the bud of her sex, circling, and her body undulated against him. Her hips moved, rotated, her body flexed. He caressed her, then dipped inside, and she tightened around him. Her mouth on his was ravenous.

He took her that way, his fingers pumping inside her, then sliding out to stroke the tight nub, back and forth, teasing, then in earnest. Her breath panted against his lips. He tweaked her nipple once more, hard. And her body released, shuddering, rocking, driving his fingers deeper. He wrapped an arm across her back and held her down, forcing her to take more, to ride the cataclysm as long as she could. Her climax rippled through his body, until his erection felt like concrete, hard and ready, crazy for her.

Slowly the orgasm subsided, and she settled against him like a blanket, boneless, her hair fragrant against his face, his hand still solidly between her legs.

"I like your orders," she muttered.

"I like the way you come." With everything in her, as if she was lost to his touch. "So what's my next lesson?"

She half-laughed, half-snorted against his neck. "You do know you're way past needing lessons. You thought up that whole giving-orders routine yourself."

"So women like to be ordered around?"

"Sometimes. In the bedroom." He felt her chuckle vibrate in his chest. "Or the backseat of a car."

Darlene hadn't. He cursed her name popping into his thoughts. "Not all women."

"No. Some are control freaks. But then sometimes you have to surprise them by taking control. And sometimes you have to let them take control."

"How do I know when to use which technique?" He didn't want to let her up. He loved the feel of her body surrounding him, his hand captured between her thighs, the cream of her arousal all over him. He'd never experienced anything more sensual in his life. For her, it was so unconscious. She was sensuality itself.

"Well," she said, shifting against him, sliding to the side. "You have to read her signals." She rose slightly, reaching down between them, dislodging his hand, and placing her own over the ridge in his pants. "Now when a woman does this, she's telling you she wants something."

"What do you want?" He couldn't breathe, let alone think of the right question.

She reached down with both hands this time and tugged on his belt. "When I do this"—she unzipped his slacks and slipped her hand inside—"it means I want to control *this*." She squeezed him, and his head felt like it might pop its cork, both heads, in fact.

"And how do you control it?"

She smiled like the devil herself. "Let me show you," she whispered.

A breeze washed over him through the open car windows as she slid sideways. Wrapping her hand around him, she revealed everything. "This is your power." She leaned down and swiped her tongue over his crown.

He shuddered, his body wanting to force its way deep into her mouth.

"When I do this…" She slid down fast on him, her lips caressing him all the way to his base and back up until his breath simply stopped in his chest. "I'm suddenly the one with the power."

He gulped air, but he couldn't say a word because she'd stolen his power of speech as well.

"Feel all that power." She tightened her fist around him and took him deep into her mouth again. Up, down, twice more, and his hands were clenched, one around her thigh, the other in her hair.

"And taste all that power." She looked up at him, her eyes the deep blue of midnight. "Women like power." She squeezed and teased with her lips and tongue, licking and sucking his crown, her hand caressing his shaft. "We like it when we believe you'll do anything, say anything just so we won't stop."

Oh yeah, he'd beg. He'd say anything she wanted. "God, yes, please. Do it."

"That's a good boy," she whispered, and then she demolished him.

Power coursed through Jordana. He was salty and sweet, thick and hard, his skin like silk against her lips. His body trembled, and his groans vibrated against her as she leaned on him. She loved this act, everything about it, all the tastes, the scents, the feel of hard flesh. She loved being the only thing a man could think about in that moment. Grady was all hers, his hand fisted in her hair, his fingers digging into her thigh, holding her there as she possessed him completely.

His body quaked, and she knew his explosion was coming. She worked him harder, faster, pushing him closer to the edge. Until he groaned and his stomach clenched, and she tasted all of him.

She held him down the way he'd held her as she'd lost herself to him on her living room floor. She pushed him over the edge and let him fly, glorying in every sound, a grunt, a groan, a curse, a deep growl.

And then he laughed. "Jesus, you make me crazy."

She lingered a few moments longer, feeling the involuntary jerks of his body. Then she patted him down, zipped his pants, and crawled up against him.

He sucked in his breath, shot it out, and tightened his arm around her. "I wanted to…" The words trailed off.

"Have your wicked way with me?"

He gave a breathless laugh. "Yeah. That would describe it."

"Well, here's the lesson. Sometimes, that's all a woman wants. Just to make you feel her power. Especially after what you did to me." She trailed a finger down the center of his chest. "If I'd wanted the rest, I would have stopped before."

"But what if you didn't know you held all the power?"

"Oh, I knew." She petted him. He was still half hard. "And that's exactly what I wanted."

He grabbed her chin and pulled her up to kiss her. It was a long, sweet, lingering meld of lips and tongues. And it shocked her. "I didn't think you'd kiss me after that." Some men liked the naughty nature of it, but she hadn't thought Grady would.

"You kissed me after I made you come with my mouth." He put his lips against her cheek as he said, "And I wanted to do the same. It was sexy. Everything about you is sexy and sensual and amazing."

Emotion bloomed inside her.

"I liked giving you my power." He stroked his thumb along her jaw.

Most men did, but there was something reverent in Grady's voice.

"I'm going to think about that all night long." His whisper stroked her, like his fingers in her hair or his hand on her throat. "I'm going to wake up feeling your mouth on me."

She wanted to go home with him, wanted to do everything all over again, wanted to taste him, ride him, roll him on top of her and feel his weight pinning her to the mattress.

God, she wanted everything. And it was terrifying.

He must have done something wrong. She'd pushed away, kissed him fast, and said, "Good."

Then she'd smiled, climbed out the other side of the car, and was gone before he had time to assess exactly what had happened.

He didn't move from the backseat. If anyone had driven in, they'd have been busted because there'd been nothing but Jordana, nothing but her kiss, her touch, her mouth on him.

She'd owned him.

Thoughts were pushing at his mind. His marriage, his past, the things he'd done, the ways he'd felt. And he couldn't let them in, not now, because he knew he'd never given away power like he had just now. He had never given a woman what she wanted. He had never desired anyone like this.

Jordana was teaching him more than he really wanted to know about himself.

CHAPTER FIFTEEN

Grady missed seeing Jordana outside his office. She'd been a constant presence, always on his mind. He'd done his work, hadn't shirked his duties, but she'd been there in his periphery.

The things he'd felt last night in the car made her move to the opposite corner all the more poignant.

He craved seeing her, but he didn't give in to the urge to walk past her office on some nebulous errand. He wasn't a schoolboy.

His cell rang midmorning, and his heart did a little jig. It was her. She craved him as much as he did her. Then he saw it was his mom.

"Hey, honey, how are you doing?" she twittered like a songbird when he answered.

"I'm fine. What's up?" His mom didn't usually call during the day while he was at work.

"I just wondered if you needed to talk yet. About Darlene."

He stared at his computer screen, the cursor flashing

where he'd left off in the middle of a sentence on the memo he'd been putting together. His teeth seemed to clench involuntarily as he flashed to his thoughts after Jordana left him alone in his car last night.

He hadn't even wanted to think Darlene's name. His anger hadn't dissipated, but he recognized his own culpability, his complacency, all the things he hadn't bothered to do. Yet when he thought of that man following her outside like a lovesick puppy, he wanted to hold onto his anger.

"Grady?"

"Not ready yet, Mom." He knew his voice was too curt, but he didn't have the control to temper it. If he started talking about Darlene, something would eventually come out about Jordana. It was too new. She was his. He didn't want to share anything yet. And he didn't want to face his guilt.

"Oh, honey. You need to get things off your chest. Have you talked to Darlene, tried to get her to see reason?"

He'd tried one time. "She was very final, Mom. She's not interested in counseling. It's too late for all that."

"You need to think about getting a lawyer." Wow, Mom was really jumping ahead. "Talk to your brother."

Grady glanced through the glass partition beside his door, but Ivy was concentrating on her computer. Still, he lowered his voice. "Nate's not a divorce lawyer."

"But he can make a good recommendation."

He didn't want to talk to Nate about his personal problems. Not yet. He'd be the first divorce in the family, with all the attached stigma.

"Honey, it's better to get on top of this right away

rather than let it get on top of you." His mother paused. "If you're really sure you can't work things out."

He was no longer sure if he even wanted to work it out. So much had happened in such a short period of time. His marriage seemed miles away. There was only room in his head for Jordana right now. "I know what you're saying, Mom." He just wasn't listening.

"Will you promise me one thing?" She waited for the *yes* she expected to come.

"Yeah. I will." His gut twisted with whatever she'd force him to do.

"Talk to Darlene. Give it your best shot. You don't want twenty years and everything you worked for to simply wash down the drain."

It was already circling the drain. But he promised because his mother was right. He'd given up too easily. He just didn't know if he owed anything to those past twenty years. And he wouldn't know unless he forced Darlene to really talk to him. "I will, Mom."

Phone still in his hand after he hung up, he stared through the empty doorway in front of him.

He had a lot to lose. Unless he wanted to fight hard and dirty, Darlene got half of everything. And in truth she owned half of everything. His salary wasn't that much higher than hers when she had a good commissions year. There was the house, its contents, the artwork, the cars, the investments. They'd have to sell the home they'd lived in for close to ten years. Or he could buy her out. But did he want that house? Did he want the memories?

Jesus, how had it all gone so wrong?

The only thing making it all bearable was Jordana. And she was just a passing fling. She'd already told him she didn't want anything permanent. She valued freedom. She didn't want ties, so she could leave her casual boyfriends behind when she got bored. She'd made no secret about who she was and how she felt.

He was just her man toy. When the lessons were over, she'd move on.

There was only one thing to be done. He'd have to keep begging for new lessons for as long as he could. Because he wasn't ready to let go, nowhere near.

Oh God, two days. Jordana didn't know how she'd gone that long? Monday night in Grady's car had been too delicious for words. Of course, she'd gotten a little nervous about the full extent of her addiction to him, but two days trying to ignore him had finally made her realize she didn't *want* to ignore him. She wanted to enjoy him for as long as she could.

Grady must have known it, too, because he was standing outside her apartment door when she got home Wednesday evening.

He couldn't wait to get his hands on her the moment they were inside the door, and two glorious hours later, Jordana was so deliciously sated that she couldn't move a muscle.

"God, how do you do that to me?" She moaned, smiling against his chest, which was lightly furred. She liked a man with hair, but hairy was a different issue. Grady's chest was absolutely perfect.

Of course, she couldn't let him into her bed too often. Having him here was just too good.

He shifted on the coverlet, somehow bringing her whole body into contact with the full length of his. "I have a very good teacher."

She hadn't taught the man all his tricks. Though maybe they weren't tricks at all. It was the way Grady gave himself over to her pleasure, making it all about her, holding off his own release until she'd had at least five mind-blowing climaxes.

Yes, he blew her mind. And that made her want to take risks she couldn't afford right now with Rhonda watching everything she did. That was another reason she hadn't made a date with Grady in two days.

"We really have to be careful now. Rhonda's looking for any excuse."

He chuckled. "I don't think she's got a spy outside your apartment watching to see if some besotted VP shows up on your doorstep."

She nuzzled her face against his skin. She liked his scent. She liked the way he laughed. "Besotted?"

"Totally," he agreed.

"That's a good word. Women want men to be besotted with them. It's heavy-duty desire."

"Thank you for another lesson."

She played lightly with his nipple until he flattened her hand against his chest.

"But I was talking about *at* work," she stressed.

"I haven't sexted you."

"Good boy." She missed his sexts. They got her going at midday while she waited for whatever he planned for after hours.

"I talked to Rhonda today about sharing Ivy with her. I'm confident Ivy can do both jobs, since you're taking most of your tasks with you."

She hadn't even thought of that solution. "Ivy's okay with that?"

"In fact, it was her idea. She wants more responsibility." He chuckled again. "As long as I run interference if Rhonda starts getting out of hand."

He'd be a good mediator. "What did Rhonda say? She hasn't mentioned it to me."

"You know Rhonda. If it's not her idea, she's got to find everything she can that's wrong with it." He smiled. She liked his smile, too. There was a lot to like about Grady. "But she's also thinking about her budget and she drove such a hard bargain that she only gets charged for a quarter of Ivy's time. The rest comes out of my budget."

"You know she'll take more than twenty-five percent of Ivy."

"Yeah, but I was already giving away twenty-five percent to you."

Jordana opened her mouth. He put his finger against her lips. "I'm planning a road trip for the three-day weekend. Can you take Tuesday off as well?"

She pushed up, fisting her hand on the mattress to brace herself. For a moment, she was caught by the perfect beauty of his body, his long limbs, flat stomach, muscled chest. She had to shake herself out of it and get to the point. "A road trip? Together? Are you crazy?"

He raised one slightly sarcastic brow. "You once said that a man needed to take responsibility for arranging fun, spur-of-the-moment trips."

"That was just an offhand remark." But Grady

remembered everything, and he always found a way to give her what she wanted and make it even better. A road trip. With him. They'd stay in hotel rooms. He'd be her captive audience. "And no, I can't take an extra day off. Especially not if we do it together. Someone's bound to figure that one out. Haven't you been listening to me? We have to be careful."

He was completely ignoring what she said. Well, almost. "Then we'll do it in three days." Since she wasn't sprawled across him anymore, he stacked his hands behind his head. "We'll leave early Saturday. Or if you want, we can take off after work on Friday, but there'll be all the holiday traffic trying to get out of the Bay Area."

"You're crazy. I can't just pick up and leave for the weekend. I was going to work, put my office together, catch up on stuff while no one was around." She hadn't even remembered it was the Labor Day weekend.

"Were you really?" he drawled, trailing a finger between her breasts, down to her abdomen, then letting his hand rest on her thigh. His touch made her want to forget everything but him.

"Well, I probably would have," she grumbled.

"Let's do this instead." He circled his fingers on the sensitive skin of her thigh.

A road trip. She liked the spontaneity of it, just pick up and drive. She liked the idea of sitting beside him for hours, plying him with questions, touching him, maybe taking advantage of him. "We'd never find a hotel at this short notice on a holiday weekend."

"You want the man to plan everything, so let me figure it out." His hand on her never stopped seducing her, mesmerizing her.

"But where would we go?"

"Leave that to me, too. I promise to make it good."

God, yes, he'd make it good. They'd sleep together, wake up together. And since this was almost like a lesson, it wouldn't be crossing a boundary. It would be like their role-play.

Whoa, did she ever know how to rationalize. But he made her want it. It was just three days and only two nights. She could handle it. Ultimately everything was about getting his wife back. That was inevitable. The end was inevitable. And she'd handle that, too.

For right now, she wanted him. And she didn't care how crazy it was.

She was this close. He almost had her. He wanted, needed, craved her agreement.

He hadn't called Darlene. He hadn't called his brother for the name of a divorce lawyer. He was in the moment with Jordana. She was all that existed right now. Everything else could wait.

Grady rolled to his side, letting his hand slide higher up her thigh. He splayed his fingers, his thumb perilously close to her center.

"Don't think," he murmured. "Just say yes. Be wild and crazy with me."

He eased closer, his thumb invading her slippery folds. His mouth watered. He wanted to taste her again, make her cry out his name.

"Grady," she whispered.

"I'll make it good for you." He thumbed her hot button and she shivered. "Come with me. Say yes." Then he bent his head to her. With all her sounds and her breathy moans, she'd taught him exactly what she loved. He put his tongue right where she needed it.

She grabbed his head, shoving her fingers through his hair. He loved it when she cried out his name, loved how her body shuddered and clamped down on him, loved her sexy wail of pleasure.

"You don't fight fair." She sucked in breath, then groaned. Finally she flopped back on the bed and her legs fell open. "All right, yes, I'll go. Oh God, yes."

And Grady took long delicious minutes sending her to heaven over and over again.

"I can't believe you made me get up at four-thirty in the morning on a holiday weekend," Jordana grumbled, her eyes still closed. But she'd done it just the same.

They hadn't spent the night together, and rather than risk the heavy commute traffic on Friday, Grady had picked her up at five on Saturday morning. He'd thrown her overnight case along with the hiking boots he'd told her to bring in the trunk and hustled her into the car. They'd set off with a mocha coffee drink from a twenty-four-hour Starbucks, and after finishing it, she'd promptly nodded off, sleeping for four hours. Now she was awake. And all his.

"I wanted to miss the traffic." His strategy had worked. They were almost two-thirds of the way to their destination, which he still hadn't revealed to her.

"Can we stop?"

Headed north on Highway 5, he pulled off at the next exit and turned into another Starbucks where they used the restrooms and ordered more coffee. Little more than five minutes later, they were back in the car.

He wasn't tired; he was energized. Because he was with her.

"Hungry?" He pointed to the lunch cooler behind his seat.

"You packed a lunch?" Jordana grabbed the insulated bag and unzipped it. She looked at him and laughed. "You made sandwiches. I can't believe it. Look at all this stuff. You're too much, Mr. Masterson."

Darlene would have made him stop at a restaurant for a sit-down meal. But he enjoyed the simple pleasures, like eating on the road.

He'd tried to think of everything that would please Jordana. Last night he'd made tuna fish and egg salad sandwiches, cut up apples, thrown in a few slices of cheese, a couple of bananas, some cherry tomatoes, and a bag of trail mix. He'd planned to start feeding her the fruit first, then the trail mix, and finally the sandwiches, but he hadn't expected her to sleep so long.

"You want tuna or egg salad?" she asked.

"We can share. Let me have half a tuna first."

She handed him one and started in on hers. "God, you make good tuna. I haven't had one of these since my mother used to make them for my lunch at school."

He realized he didn't know a damn thing about her.

Now at least he knew she had a mother who made tuna fish sandwiches.

"So when do I get to know where we're going?"

"We're going to Klamath Falls."

She gaped. "You mean in Oregon? That's like an all-day drive."

"Only seven hours with no traffic and only a few stops. We'll be there by noon." There'd been hardly any cars when they left, and even now they were moving along at a little above the speed limit.

He glanced at her to see her smile spread slowly across her face. "You're very exact. And you planned all this yourself with no help?"

"No help."

"What are we going to do in Klamath Falls?"

"That's the surprise." He had plans, probably packing in far more than they could accomplish, but they could stop whenever they got tired. Darlene had always said he overbooked their time, but then she hated it when he didn't plan at all. And why the hell did he have to keep thinking about her, comparing her?

"So tell me about your mom," he asked, just to stop the comparison game. "Is she in the area?"

Jordana handed him half the egg salad sandwich. "She's in L.A."

"How'd you come to be up here?"

"I got accepted into San Francisco State. And I liked it so much I didn't want to go back to L.A."

"And your dad?"

She turned away from him, looking out the window. "He left us when I was three. I don't know what happened to him."

That explained a lot about her, the way she liked her relationships to be short and to have the least impact on her life.

She pointed out the window. "Look at all the ducks in the canal."

He glanced past her, but had already missed the ducks. A wide canal of water fed the agricultural fields spreading out for miles on either side of the highway. He knew she was changing the subject, and he let her. "I believe the canal is part of the water reclamation project started back in the early part of the last century. The government wanted to turn the area into agricultural land to attract settlers. It goes all the way up into Oregon as well."

"Well, aren't you a fountain of information."

He had to look at her to make sure she wasn't making fun of him. He liked facts. Darlene had always been bored with his penchant to read up on a place for more than just the tourist attractions.

What did Jordana think?

Maybe he should have planned their road trip the way Darlene would have wanted it. She required fancy restaurants and spas and massages and pampering. He'd succumbed, even enjoyed himself, and now it could have been mere orneriness that he insisted on doing it his way, with the sandwiches, getting up early, and the things he'd planned for them to do, all of which Darlene would have hated.

But Jordana wasn't Darlene. Jordana was completely unique. With her, everything was different.

"Do you want to know the population of Klamath Falls?" He waited.

Jordana leaned close, her sweet scent clouding up the car. "Tell me everything you know, Mr. Masterson. All your little facts make me hot."

CHAPTER SIXTEEN

Grady was amazing. He knew something about everything and was full of interesting little factoids that made the miles fly by. Grady was smart, and that made him entertaining. He was the kind of guy who could settle into a deep conversation with just about anyone at a dinner party. A handy trait, it also steered him away from the topic of her father. She had no desire to talk about a man she couldn't even remember and didn't want to.

They passed Shasta Lake, which was down by 30 percent with the drought. She'd never seen so much parched, brown earth.

"I remember houseboating on Shasta with some friends when I was in college," she said as they crossed the bridge over the lake, a dotting of houseboats far below. "We could stop along the shore and get right out to hike in the trees." Now it would be like mountain climbing.

"Hopefully we'll have a monster *El Niño* this year."

"As long as it's not *El Wimpo* like last year," she muttered.

Grady laughed. "I haven't heard that one before. So tell me more about houseboating. Did you do a lot of wild and crazy things in college?"

She snorted a laugh. "Houseboating wasn't wild and crazy. It was eight girls who didn't know what the heck we were doing, me included."

"But I bet you had a helluva lot of fun."

She smiled, remembering how they'd almost rammed another houseboat full of college boys. Then, wanting to sunbathe on the shore, they'd come close to beaching the houseboat. The same group of boys had helped them push it back out. "We did have quite a party."

"And what nasty little thing did you do?"

She clucked her tongue. "What do you mean?"

"I can tell. You get a glint."

"You're driving. You can't even see my eyes, let alone a glint."

"But you did do something, didn't you?"

He had her figured out, she had to admit. "Just a hot boy on a moonlit night." The scenery flashed by them. Grady passed the trucks on their northward trek, and though he was over the speed limit, other cars blasted by them.

"Did you ever see him again?"

"They were from Oregon. A long way from San Francisco." Besides, she wasn't interested in a relationship. "So let's put you in the hot seat. Tell me everything there is to know about Grady Masterson."

"Nothing particularly hot in my past."

"Here's a treat if you tell me all your secrets." She gave him a handful of trail mix from the bag. "There must have been some naughty affairs with a few sexy cheerleaders in high school." She couldn't believe he'd been a virgin until he met his wife. "I bet you were a hot stud all the girls were after."

He shot out a laugh. "I was a nerd." He ate the handful of nuts and raisins even though he wasn't giving her much information.

"No way."

"Yes, way. I did manage to get a girlfriend. She was in the school band back when being in the band wasn't cool."

"Ooh, poor baby. An uncool girlfriend. Let me give you an apple to make up for it." She held out the bag of sliced apples, and he took two. She liked learning these snippets about him. "So what happened to the girl in the band?"

He ate one apple slice before answering. "We went to different colleges. I stayed local and she went to Humboldt."

"Where did you go?"

"Santa Clara University."

She was pretty sure that wasn't a cheap state school. Not that any school was cheap these days.

"You didn't want to go away?"

"We all went to Santa Clara. My parents liked the idea of us being close."

"We?" She wanted to glean more facts. She wanted to know how he met his wife, but she wasn't about to bring that up.

"I've got three brothers and a sister. All younger than me."

"Wow. I have no idea what it's like to have so many siblings." She had no idea what it was like to have a family or a father.

"It's a freaking nightmare. Especially now that I've got nieces and nephews as well." He made it sound bad, but she recognized his fond smile. She wanted to ask why he'd never had kids, but again, it felt like a taboo subject. Anything to do with his wife was, especially when they were on a role-play road trip.

"We have a family dinner once a month." He gave her the whole rundown, what each of his brothers did, a lawyer, a tax accountant with his own firm, an engineer. Only one of them was married, the lawyer. His sister was a homemaker. And his mom sounded like June Cleaver from that old fifties show, the icon who wore pearls while she vacuumed.

"What about your mom? What does she do?"

The question threw her off balance. Her mother was the antithesis of Grady's. Jordana's life growing up was, too. Single mother, absent father. "She's a bartender."

"That's interesting." It was the most diplomatic thing he could say, Jordana was sure.

"Yeah. She worked nights." And she liked to sample. "She worked hard to put me through college." Jordana had also gotten a scholarship and worked to pay all her expenses. "I asked her if she wanted to move up here when I did, but she likes it down there." She'd asked out of familial duty, even politeness. Her mother had simply given her a look that said it all.

She decided she was done with the whole topic. "So are you going to tell me exactly what you've got planned for our trip?"

"I want to show you Crater Lake."

She'd never been there. She'd never even seen pictures.

Like a travel guide, Grady proceeded to tell her all the relevant facts and history. "The water is the most amazing blue you'll ever see. It's all mountain runoff."

They passed through the town of Weed, and he turned off Highway 5 onto a smaller road, driving them through fields of waving grass that ended abruptly in a heavily burned area.

"I wonder when they had the fire," she wondered.

"I'm not sure."

She turned on him. "Something you don't know? I'm shocked."

He tipped his head at her, looking over the rim of his sunglasses. "Are you mocking me?"

"No. I love that you're such a know-it-all."

"Right."

She leaned over, stretching her seatbelt, and kissed him on the cheek. Then she couldn't resist licking his ear.

"We're going to have an accident if you don't stop."

"Didn't anyone ever do naughty things to you while you were driving?" She put her palm on his pants. "On my. I think you're hard." Her mouth suddenly salivated for a taste of him.

He covered her hand, pressed. Then he growled. "You would be my first. But would I be yours?"

She blew in his ear, squeezed him a little tighter. "No. I've been a very naughty girl. Maybe you should punish me tonight."

"I'm going to have to."

He would let her do it now, she knew, take him in her mouth, make him crazy. She might even be able to get him to beg for it. She could have all the power just as she'd had in his car a few days ago. But suddenly she didn't want

Grady to be like every other man. She didn't want him to beg. She didn't want to be the only one with the power.

"Yes," she whispered. "I'm sure you're going to need to punish me." She subsided into her seat.

"Tease," he said.

"No. I'm just saving it for later."

He glanced at her as the burned landscape fell away behind them. "What if I want it now?"

"What if I tell you it'll be so much better when we do it together?"

He leaned over to cup her core between her legs. "You're hot."

"I'm wet, too," she told him, her body arching into his touch.

"Then we'll need a soundproof room because I'm going to make you scream."

"Promise?"

He smiled, a wicked, devilish grin that made her melt against his hand. "Oh yeah, I promise. I'll make you scream until you think you're going to faint."

And he would do it. He was the best any woman had ever had.

It would have been so easy and so damn good to beg her to put her mouth on him, to take him and drain every drop. Grady had wanted it so damn badly he'd been willing to risk an accident. But more, he wanted to hold back until they were both crazy with need. Getting off in the moment would have been way too easy. He wanted this to be as good as he could get, as good as they both could get.

He'd planned these two nights with her. It was a huge step, but he didn't care. He wanted it, needed it, her in his bed all night long. When she was gone, he would savor the memories.

So he kept driving, kept asking her questions, trying to learn everything about her. But she was cagey, and he revealed far more than he learned. All he knew was that her mother was a bartender in an upscale bar somewhere in L.A., that she'd had Jordana when she was twenty, been dumped when she was twenty-three, left with a toddler to raise on her own. She'd done a fabulous job. That was his own conclusion, not something Jordana passed on.

He'd originally planned to go to the hotel in Klamath Falls first, but they were too early to actually get a room. So he'd called the front desk to say they'd be a late check-in, then drove straight up to Crater Lake. There were several hours of daylight, more than enough to make it around the park, and with only a three-day trip, he didn't want to waste the little time they had.

The lake was as blue as he'd promised, and the park was crowded on the last long weekend of the season. The boat rides were already full for all three days, but they'd taken the mile-long switchback down to the lake to test the waters, which were cold enough to freeze a man's privates even in the late summer heat.

Jordana, of course, stripped down to the swimsuit she'd donned in the backseat of the car while he played lookout. She'd screamed when she plunged in.

It wasn't the kind of scream he'd make sure she gave him later, but he loved her childlike exuberance, her laughter, the way she wanted to try everything. She'd even made him stop along the way around the lake so she could climb to the top of a roadside waterfall.

Jordana was glued to the view out her window throughout the entire drive, even once they were headed back to Klamath Falls. Granted it was long after the dinner hour, but the downtown was still extraordinarily empty, especially for a holiday.

Large pots of brightly colored flowers hung from lampposts along the wide, clean main street of the old town. Many of the stores had been renovated, and the old bank buildings had been turned into restaurants, coffee shops, and bars. But there were also derelict buildings, boarded-up hotels, and an abandoned Ford dealership with stucco facsimiles of Egyptian kings on the front and sides that appeared recently repainted as if for a restoration that ran out of money. On a hill above the main street, the old high school looked deserted and under reconstruction, its surrounding trees chopped down to stumps.

Finding a parking space along the one-way street wasn't a problem, and he took Jordana's hand in his as they strolled along the sidewalk. "Where would you like to eat?"

She glanced down at their clasped hands. He liked the feel of her skin against his, the warmth spreading up his arm. They were all about sex, and yet somehow this felt like more than sex.

For a moment, he expected her to pull away, but then she said, "Wherever. I don't mind."

There were no lines anywhere, no crowds spilling out onto the sidewalk. They passed a Mexican place with a standard menu listed on a signboard outside. Voices and music drifted from the open doors of what had once been yet another bank building.

He figured it was a better bet than the Chinese place without a single diner inside. The only occupant seemed to be waiting for take-out. "Let's try Mexican."

"Sounds good. I'm dying for a margarita."

Grady pulled Jordana beneath his arm, his fingers playing through her hair. It felt too damn good to touch her this way, with familiarity, almost ownership, so different than sex, yet so intimate. She didn't shrug him off.

They were seated in a booth in the large main dining room decorated in a zebra motif.

"They're watching us," Jordana whispered. There were zebra pictures, zebra statues, some with necks as long as a giraffe, small paper-mache zebras, a zebra-print rug hanging on the wall. "It's kind of weird to see them in a Mexican place."

The margaritas, however, came in the requisite cactus-shaped glasses, and the food was hot and spicy. The place wasn't full by any means, but at least half the tables were occupied, which was more than he could say for the Chinese place. A mariachi band played softly through speakers, covering up any nearby conversations, masking theirs as well, but at least they didn't have to shout over too loud music and too many voices. He preferred it to the bar on University Avenue.

"I'd love to stay at the Crater Lake Lodge." Jordana's face was slightly pink from the heat of the salsa dip. "That view was fabulous. It would be so cool in the winter time."

He tapped his phone and opened the browser, typing in the lodge. "It's closed in winter." He clicked a link, then he laughed. "And it recommends you book a year in advance."

She crossed her eyes at him. "You're such a spoilsport. Let me have my dream."

He opened his mouth to say he'd love to take her next year. His fingers itched to make the reservation now. But Jordana was temporary. She didn't want anything permanent or long-term. He wished he'd added a codicil to the road trip, one that said they were to pretend for the duration that they were a couple, that they had a relationship. But he hadn't said that.

So he let his own dream die.

At least she would be in his bed tonight, and she'd wake up beside him in the morning. It was all he could ask for.

After dinner, she made him order flan for dessert, and it tasted as sweet as she did.

She leaned forward to say, "I've got a brilliant idea."

He felt a prickle of heat rising in him. She had such good brilliant ideas.

"Let's do another role-play." Her voice was low, seducing him from the inside out.

"What do you have in mind?" She already had him. He'd do anything.

"We'll pretend we don't know each other, and you're going to try to pick me up in a bar."

"But you do already know me."

"This will teach you the approach."

"Will it be anything like the young lady who wanted a ménage?"

"Of course not," she scoffed. "I told you I didn't plan that one. She just showed up, and you charmed her immediately."

He still wondered if she'd had a hand in it despite all her denials. "I have no idea how to pick you up when I already know you."

She sighed and rolled her eyes. "You sit down at the bar and you start looking around. You see me and you see if you can catch my eye. Then you send a drink to my table."

"That sounds too easy."

Propping her chin on her hands, she looked at him. Until finally she said, "Maybe someone else will try to pick me up, and you'll have to beat him out."

He would definitely have to do some beating if anyone else came near her.

"Or maybe I refuse your drink and you have to try harder."

"You wouldn't refuse my margarita. You like them too much."

She shook her head sadly. "I could buy my own, you know." Then she widened her eyes at him and pursed her lips. "Do you want to play or not?"

"Oh yeah. I want to play."

Jordana would make it good no matter how it played out. And he was dying to discover what she'd do.

CHAPTER SEVENTEEN

Jordana was so damn sexy in her short jeans skirt, her legs crossed. Just before looking for a bar, she'd dug in her small suitcase for a pair of high heels. They made his blood rush. Her orange tank top bared her shoulders and the creamy skin of her throat. It was cut low enough to showcase the succulent swell of her breasts. More blood flooded his extremities. Her hair cascaded over her shoulders and back, and he dreamed of burying his face in all that silk. She made his mouth water, and he gulped down two swallows of margarita.

Every unattached guy in the place had his eye on her.

Grady had already decided he wouldn't be the first to approach her. She was sensual, beautiful, and gave off the aura of being totally comfortable in her skin. He wanted to see how many bees she would attract to her honey. Before he had to beat them off.

For the few cars parked along Main Street, every single one of their drivers must have been in this bar. The music was a loud country rock that screeched in his ears, but the men were dressed like loggers in flannel shirts and backward baseball caps. A Karaoke set-up was ready to go against the far wall but lacked any takers. A rowdy group of girls in the corner celebrated the twenty-first birthday of a redhead with an unfortunately blotchy face. But she was having a damn good time, and the drinks kept flowing. He hoped she had a designated driver.

From his seat on a bar stool, he'd only looked away a second, and some sleazeball had already slid into the seat next to Jordana. The man, younger than Grady, more Jordana's age, held out a second margarita to match hers. Gazing briefly at Grady with the slightest of smirks, she tapped the rim of her glass, then covered it with her hand. She was blowing the guy off.

Wait, wrong choice of words. It reminded him of Monday night in the backseat of his car. His gut roiled at the thought of Jordana doing that to anyone but him.

The dejected clodhopper, his bushy head wagging disappointedly, lumbered back to his table of buddies, taking the margarita with him. Out of politeness, he should have left it with her. His friends commiserated with claps on his back.

Grady watched her, considering the right time to make his move. His heart rate was up already, just from one attempted pickup. How many more could he take?

Glass in hand, eyes on him, Jordana licked salt from the rim, then followed it with a margarita chaser. That swipe of her tongue was enough to send his heart into overdrive, beating so hard he could feel it send blood rushing through his ears. And down to other parts as well.

Was that how a woman signaled to a man what she wanted?

What signal had Darlene given that she wanted to cheat?

He immediately cursed himself for the thought even as a rush of anger bubbled through his veins along with everything else. This was about Jordana. This was about him being smooth enough to talk her into leaving the bar with him. It was another test, another lesson. He wouldn't fail with Jordana.

One crossed leg swung, her high heel enticing him. Then she stroked a finger along the neck of her tank top, stopping just short of touching her breast. Hell, she was a tease, sending him out of control. She was a firecracker ready to go off, ready to make him explode right along with her.

Before he could decide that enough was enough, another man plopped down in the chair next to her, pulling it even closer, leaning in, his legs almost bracketing her swinging foot. He wore the scruffy two-day beard women seemed so fond of.

Grady went a little crazy and thought about smashing the guy. But, of course, he was nonviolent.

Jordana glanced at Grady, so quick he almost missed it, and the pick-up man certainly didn't notice. She pointedly looked at her glass, which was half full—or half empty depending on whether she wanted to accept a second margarita.

She toyed with the rim, then licked the salt off her finger. She was playing a dangerous game. If she didn't shoo the guy away, Grady would have to do something drastic. He might just have to drag her out of here.

Finally she pushed the offered glass away and shook her head, scooting her chair back out of his range.

Grady thought there might be a problem and put one foot on the floor. But then the man pushed his chair back, too, his face reddened beneath the scruff, and stomped away, leaving the margarita with Jordana.

She looked at him. They eye-flirted. The music seemed to get louder, beating on the inside of his skull. His jeans were tighter, his body a hard ache for her. He hadn't ordered another drink yet. He'd been too busy watching her. But it was time, past time if he didn't want to lose her to some jerk who was younger, taller, smooth-talking, with a broad chest in a GQ suit. He was actually feeling it, the role-play, like there was a chance another man would beat him to her. Anger and a taste of fear welled up. He raised a hand to signal the bartender.

It was already too late.

The guy that sat beside her wore acres of hard-working manly flannel to cover all those muscles. His clean-shaven face was something out of one of those hunky firefighter calendars women loved. He was big, with massive thighs in a pair of jeans accompanied by heart-stomping boots. He was the Brawny Man come to life.

Jordana seemed to be melting into a puddle of mush right before him.

The guy pushed the other man's margarita out of the way, then snapped his fingers for the bartender to bring her a fresh one. And the barman actually rushed to do his bidding.

Jordana laughed, a sexy, husky, tie-your-guts-in-knot laugh. A jealous burn started low in Grady's belly, rising up his body to his throat. The guy was too close but she didn't pull away. No, she seemed hypnotized, her gaze on all those muscles, and then his mouth. She didn't make eye contact with Grady, didn't even turn her head. As if he didn't exist.

Well, screw that. She wasn't walking away from him so easily. He'd learned what women craved. They needed to be desired, and desire for her was a gnawing, roiling ache crimping his insides. He wasn't the complacent vanilla hack he'd been a month ago. He knew the secret of the perfect sexy kiss, knew exactly where to touch her, how to make her scream and cry out his name.

Then she leaned in and said something to the man.

That was it. Grady saw the red haze they talked about in books but he'd never really believed in. It came down over his eyes, tinging everything around him and bathing her in its red glow. His fists balled, and suddenly his feet were planted on the plank floor.

No damn way was he letting her walk out on him with some beefcake wearing enough muscles to make women drool. She wasn't leaving here with anyone but him.

The man was impressive. If she'd never met Grady, she would have let this one buy her a drink. She might have let him do more.

But there was Grady. How long was it going to take for him to pick her up? They'd been playing eye footsie for what seemed like hours, through all the men who'd tried to give her drinks.

What was taking him so long? She refused to give

him the eye again. She'd already sent him enough cues.

"Do you do Karaoke?" the man said. He'd told her his name, but the music was too loud and she hadn't asked him to repeat it.

She leaned in and said, "What?" Because she couldn't believe that was his pickup line.

He didn't have time to answer. The floor rumbled and the room tilted and a fire-breathing Grady towered over them, his face a hard mask of cold anger.

"So you didn't think I'd figure out what you were up to when you left the house all dressed up in your pretty high heels." His voice was low, soft, and deadly.

Her mouth dropped open, and she couldn't seem to shut it.

"Nothing to say for yourself?" His voice was so sharp it could crack ice. "You think I wouldn't figure out you were cheating?"

"Hey, buddy," her new Karaoke friend started.

Grady turned on him, pointed his index finger. "Get lost. My wife's not interested."

She put a hand to her mouth because she suddenly wanted to laugh. He was role-playing the heavy husband. And she found it pretty darn hot, her body already reacting to him.

Mr. Karaoke stood, holding his hands up. "Didn't know she was taken." Then he backed away slowly, like a meek storekeeper faced with a gunslinger.

"She's taken, all right," Grady snarled. He was good, really good.

He hauled the chair right up next to her and sat, his face right in hers. "So I'm not good enough in bed," he said with that same deadly softness.

She played along. "No. It's not that."

"Right. So you're cheating because I'm the best you've ever had and you just want to see how others compare?" The bar was dim, but Grady's face was even darker.

"No, sweetie, it's not like that."

"Don't lie to me," he said through gritted teeth. "I'm not an idiot."

She ran her gaze over him, taking in his handsome features, the lips she'd kissed. She didn't know what set him off. Maybe it was the men who'd brought her drinks. Maybe it was just the way a mind could jump from one thing to another then another and suddenly spiral down. He was role-playing but this wasn't about her. It was about his wife, about what she'd done to him, not just cheating, but tearing a hole in his manhood, showing him he wasn't good enough, had never been good enough.

She wanted to touch him, tell him he'd never done anything wrong. But he was untouchable, and she ached with helplessness, ached with wanting to soothe him. "You're the best," she whispered.

"Don't try buttering me up. You've got one choice to make." His hard gaze bored right into her heart. "Or consider it over."

He'd given his wife a choice. And she'd walked away.

Jordana wasn't about to make the same mistake. "I'll go with you."

She expected the role-play to end, for the real Grady to come back, but he narrowed his eyes and said, "Good choice."

His chair scraped on the wood floor as he pushed it back. They stood together, and Jordana realized they were center stage. They were the Saturday night fight up on the big screen. Grady threw bills on the table to cover their drinks, then he propelled her out with his hand at her back.

No one tried to stop them.

She shivered as they stepped out onto the sidewalk. The temperature had dropped slightly, but it was this strange Grady that sent a thrill through her. She could feel the heat of his pulse through his fingers. His skin was hot, his emotion palpable. He was like a wounded predator lashing out, and while it tripped up her heart, it also made him exciting and different and unknowable.

What did he plan next?

Grabbing her hand, he pulled her down the street to his car. She almost had to run to keep up.

He unlocked the door, opened it. "Get in." Then he slammed it hard, rounded the hood, and climbed in on the other side. His tires squealed as he took off, the powerful engine racing as fast as her heart.

"Grady."

"Don't say a word."

She shut her mouth. He was vibrating, his intensity humming in the car's interior.

He turned a corner, then turned again, gunned the motor, and they raced to the edge of downtown where he took a left, up and over a bridge to the darkened school. There wasn't a single light in the parking lot, just the moon. The logs of the felled trees lay in piles, and he steered around them, finally yanking the wheel to turn in between two stacks and braking to a hard stop.

"Get in the backseat," he ordered, and her heart beating wildly, she climbed through the seats while he opened his door. Then he was beside her, suddenly on her.

"Is this what you want?" he said, his voice harsh. "Some guy who can't wait to get his hands on you." He pushed her skirt to her waist, spread her legs, and slid between them. "You want some guy who's so crazy for you he's gotta have it now, right now, right here in the backseat?" He was thick and hard, and he ground against her.

"Grady." She arched, everything inside her wet and hot for him. Yet she felt his pain in every word, in his hands on her, in the relentless hardness of his body. He hadn't done right, hadn't been enough, hadn't felt enough. And there was only one way to make him feel better.

"You want me to be totally nuts for you?" he growled at her.

"Yes. God, yes." She needed it so badly she couldn't even beg. She could only moan her need for him.

He held her head, brought his mouth down on hers, and completely consumed her. He was everything she tasted, everything she breathed, everything she touched.

He tore her panties aside, slid his fingers inside her. She groaned into his mouth.

"Is this what you want?" he whispered against her lips.

"I want you. You make me so crazy and wild." She had to let him know how perfect he was.

He played her, inside and out, stroking her from the edge of her sex, then as deep as he could go.

"Is this enough desire? Is this good enough? Are you going to pretend to yourself that another's man doing this to you?"

His pain lashed her. His need set loose a deep ache

inside. What had his wife done to him? All Jordana wanted to do was fix it for him, show him that he was like no other man. "Only you, Grady," she said on her next moan. "I only want you, think about you, dream about you. Don't stop. Please."

"You want me inside you? Is that what you need?"

"Yes, Grady, please." Then she was out of control, pulling him, squirming to get closer.

He shoved up then, diving a hand into his pocket. The brightly colored condom packet sparkled in the sliver of moonlight through the back window. He tore it, rolled it on, amazing her with how good at it he'd become.

Then he was poised between her legs. "Is this what you want me to be? So crazy for you that I'll screw you in the backseat because I can't wait one more second to have you?"

He didn't wait. Not one single second. He plunged deep, and she cried out his name, her fingernails biting into his arms as she held him.

"God, I want you. Jesus, I need you." His breath panted against her ear.

He took her hard enough to ram her up against the car door. She braced a hand there, pushed back on him. It was wild, crazy, out of control, and she started to come almost immediately, her body convulsing around him. It could have been seconds, it could have been minutes, it could have been forever. Then his body went rigid, he growled deep in his throat, thrust high and hard inside her two more times and held tight to her, his legs and arms quaking.

Her ears were ringing as their bodies quieted. He throbbed lightly, then even that stopped.

"You make me crazy," he whispered into her hair.

She held him tight, legs wrapped around him. He'd given her exactly what she'd told him a woman wanted, given her what his wife said he'd denied her. He had nothing left to prove.

Her lips against his ear, she breathed the words into him. "You're the best there ever was."

Until this moment, she hadn't understood what his wife had done to him, how badly she'd hurt him, how much she'd stripped from him.

Jordana wanted to give it all back.

"How many gold stars?" he murmured.

"More than I can count."

He shifted. "Did I pass Role-play One-oh-one?"

"You were incredible." She laughed against his hair. "I thought you might actually beat that guy up."

"I'm nonviolent." He turned, started to rise, pulling her with him until she was straddling him. "But I did feel pushed to the limit with all those men drooling over you."

She stroked his hair, smoothing it down. "That was totally hot, the way you dragged me out of there."

"I can play the he-man."

Her heart was still thrumming, emotion riding in her throat. The sex had been good, but something momentous had happened. They'd been connected. They'd fed on each other's desire. She'd taken his pain into herself and eaten it away, made him better, soothed his pain.

Sex had never been about comfort, about erasing someone else's ache. It had just been physical, just sex. But Grady made it different. He made it… intimate.

Cupping his face in her hands, she held him, forcing him to look at her, willing him to understand. "You know everything now."

His eyes traced her features. "Do I?"

"Yes, you absolutely do."

"Kiss me one more time," he whispered. "Because we better get out of here in case the cops patrol this place."

She laughed against his mouth. "You're such a risk-taker." Then she took his lips and gave him a piece of her heart and soul in their kiss.

CHAPTER EIGHTEEN

She slept in his arms, her hair fragrant against his face, her body soft and warm. Grady hadn't thought much about heaven, but this must be it. Jordana breathed gently and rhythmically. He felt every rise and fall of her body against his. Her taste still teased his senses.

He hadn't planned what happened in the bar or what he'd done in the car afterward. He'd simply lost it. The thought of that guy touching her had sent his guts into a tailspin. After that, all he'd wanted to do was prove he was better, that she couldn't live without him, that no other man could occupy a space in her mind or her body, that he was the *only* one. He didn't want to own her, but nor could he stand the thought of sharing her. He couldn't abide returning to work on Tuesday and becoming just another executive she had to service, like Rhonda or Brett.

But dammit, laying in the dark with the feel of her all over him, he didn't want to think about Tuesday or anything else.

He hadn't made love to her in the car. He'd simply

taken her, hard, fast, and so good that his throat had seized up with his own need. He hadn't even felt like himself. Hell, no, he'd been better. He'd been exactly what Jordana wanted.

And yet, when they returned to the hotel, he'd planned on making it right, touching her the way she deserved. But Jordana had fallen asleep before he'd even stepped out of the bathroom. The drive had been long, then the exertion of climbing around Crater Lake, and finally their nocturnal activities had taken their toll. So he'd crawled into the king bed completely naked. He'd never slept naked in his life, though God only knew why now that he'd discovered the heavenly feel of skin against skin. *Her* skin against his.

And for now, she was his all night long.

There were so many things Jordana made him see, so many things she'd taught him to feel.

He didn't want his routines anymore. He didn't want to settle for take-out, emails, PBS, and sex once a week on Saturdays. He didn't want to settle for a woman who climaxed with him only when she was thinking of someone else.

He didn't want to *settle*.

And yet he had to settle for two nights with Jordana.

The air conditioning was on high, but the blankets were blissfully thick and heavy around her. And Grady was so warm.

There was no instant of disorientation. Jordana

simply woke, knew where she was and that it was Grady's hard body she was plastered against.

He'd listened to everything she'd told him, then planned the trip, made it fun and unexpected, and chosen the perfect venue. True, she hadn't seen much because she was tired and it was late, but the lodge had a huge fireplace that was open on two sides, giving a glow to both the lobby and the restaurant. Floor-to-ceiling windows would showcase a fabulous view of the grounds during a meal. The room itself was sumptuous with a jet tub in the bathroom, plush carpeting that soothed her feet, and an oversize bed with a thick comforter. She loved the weight of the blankets, but even more, she loved the weight of Grady.

Through the slit in the curtains, she could make out the early morning light. She'd never slept with a man. Somehow she'd always imagined it would be stifling and confining. Yet with Grady it was deliciously decadent. He was safe. She didn't have to worry that he'd ask for too much. When this was all over, he'd use his new skills on his wife and win her back to live happily ever after.

Even as the careless thought flitted through her mind, it ground her heart into shards. His wife didn't deserve him. No way, no how. In the car, as he'd raged inside her, she'd felt what that woman had done to him, how she'd crushed him. Hours later, Jordana could still feel his pain in the very pit of her belly like an ache that spread its tentacles through her whole body. She wanted to wrap herself around him, protect him, save him. How could she let him go back to that woman? Was it right? But it was sort of like Eddie. A man had to make his own decision. She'd never really liked Eddie's wife, and it had hurt when she wasn't allowed to be his friend anymore. It hurt that he'd chosen the other woman over her. But he wanted kids. He wanted a long-term *love* relationship that she would never have been able to give him.

And Grady wanted his wife back.

She snuggled deeper into his big, beautiful body. Why was she even thinking about it? She and Grady were only playing at being lovers. She was getting carried away, confusing fantasy with reality. They weren't even in a relationship, and she could never allow herself to become dependent on him. He was doing this all for his wife. After all, he'd never taken off his wedding ring. Maybe their non-relationship was even a form of therapy for him.

Yet a tiny part of her was terribly afraid the ache in her belly was actually for herself, for the day Grady decided he didn't need any more lessons, for the day he didn't need *her*.

God, she was overthinking everything. For right now, this morning, in this bed, he was her fantasy man, and she was going to enjoy the moment. She was going to indulge herself, do all the things she'd never allowed herself. Like waking up nestled against a gorgeous, hard male body. She'd fantasized about it, but she'd never had it. Now was her chance.

Beneath the covers, Jordana ran her fingers up his thigh. Grady had been awake for several minutes, enjoying her body shifting against his. But with her hand on his thigh, he was completely *awake*, his blood rushing to his center and turning him instantly rock hard.

He wanted to roll and conquer, pull her beneath him and stake his claim with elemental reaction. But he let her have her bedroom play.

She moved up his side, the molecules of his skin heating beneath her light but heady touch. She stroked his upper arm, then curved around and trailed fire across his chest, over his nipple, sending sparks straight down to his erection. He actually twitched. But still he let her have her way.

His arm was curled over his sternum, and she smoothed the backs of her fingers over and down his abdomen. Down, down, down. Until she was stroking the very essence of him with feathery touches that made his skin shiver. She dropped down even lower and cupped him, squeezing softly until he was full and ready, crazy ready.

Then her hand circled him, held him in her grip, her thumb teasing his tip, stroking the tiny pearl of moisture all over.

He could hear his heart in his ears, the overactive thump-thump beating against the drum. Everything was on fire, his blood, his skin, his muscles, his brain, his breath searing his lungs.

This was how it should have been. This was how it had never been. Until Jordana.

"Jordana." He heard the crack in his voice.

"Does it feel good?" she whispered.

"Yes. Jesus, yes." And his voice broke again.

"Do it to me."

As if they shared one mind, he understood exactly what she wanted. Rolling until he faced her, he let his hands do all the talking, just the way she had. His eyes locked on hers, which were bright even in the dim light of sun peeking through the curtains, he held her gaze as his hands roamed all her curves and valleys.

"I could do this for hours." Even as wild with need as he felt, the creamy texture of her skin against his fingers mesmerized him. He stroked her from neck to navel, from knee to the curls at her apex. He delved between her legs, but only a moment, giving himself only a taste.

"Mmm," she hummed her pleasure for him. "Now use your lips on me."

Throwing back the covers, he made love to her with his mouth, not just her erogenous zones, but every inch of skin. He licked her ear until she moaned for him, then her collarbone, the hollow at her throat. She was still salty-sweet from last night, and he savored her with his tongue. Then he lavished attention on her breasts, her nipples, her arms, the crook of her elbow, her belly button. And even then he didn't go for the gold between her sweet thighs. He licked up her legs, behind her knee, the sweet milk of her thighs.

She was writhing before he ever put his mouth between her legs. "Grady," she gasped his name, tangling her fingers in his hair, trying to drag him closer.

"I'm not done with you," he murmured against her flesh. Then he rolled her to her stomach and put his tongue to her back, up and down her spine.

She squirmed, her hands fisting in the sheets. "Oh my God. That makes me insane." She arched, pushing her delicious rump into his aching erection.

He crawled up her body, kissing and licking his way, until he covered her, nestled between the crevice of her buttocks, his lips buried against her neck. And then he simply began to move, rocking against her. She spread her legs slightly, and the friction between them was almost too much, more than he could handle. And yet he went on.

"So good," he murmured against her hair.

"Like this, Grady." She groaned and pushed up against him. "Please, like this. Right now."

The feel of her skin against him was immense. He wanted to bury himself inside her, not just her body, but her mind, her soul.

There were condoms on the bedside table, and he grabbed one, sheathed himself.

"I'm going to put a pillow under you." He'd never made love in this position—it was too crude to call it doggy style, and there was nothing crude about Jordana. He'd always been a missionary guy, a vanilla guy, sometimes letting himself be ridden, but he knew what he craved right now.

Together they shoved a pillow under her belly, raising her enough to make his entry easier. And then he slid slowly home inside her, until he was sure he could feel her womb, even her heart. He lay like that for long moments, savoring the clench of her body around him.

It was like coming home. He wanted to stay deep inside her, never leave. "I fit so good," he whispered, breathing in the citrus of her hair and the sweetness of her skin. "Does it feel good?"

"Yes." Then she laced her fingers with his. "Flex inside me."

He did. She groaned into the mattress, burying her face. Then she pushed back against him. It was heaven and hell. He wanted to take her hard and fast, ride her down in the bed. Yet he wanted the gentle luxury of her body surrounding him.

"Slow," he whispered to her. "And sweet." Then he braced himself on his arms and rocked into her. She pushed back to meet him.

"I don't know if I can take it slow, it's too good." She grunted, and he loved the way she loved the physical, the way she relished it with her sounds.

She was slick and hot around him, her body tensing on him rhythmically. He took her like that, sure, steady, and mind-blowing until his arms started to shake, until he needed to touch her even as he filled her.

This was how he wanted their two nights to be, hours of luxury and lovemaking. Hot, heavy, and fast in the car had been as sublime as slow and sweet was now.

Then she started to beg. "Please, Grady, please, Grady."

His name on her lips did something to him, released the beast inside him, taking her harder, faster, until they were both gasping. With close to his last coherent thought, he knew she was close to the peak, her body working him. He pushed his hand under her, found her little button, and played her. She didn't hold back, crying his name, and dragging him down into bliss right along with her.

He knew only one thing before everything exploded. This was nothing like vanilla. This was making love. This was what he'd needed to learn.

And Jordana had taught it to him.

Jordana could have stayed in bed the rest of the day. She could have licked and kissed every inch of his body. She could have let him do those things to her for hours, even days.

So it was a good thing that Grady insisted they get on with his plans for the day. She'd enjoyed what he'd done to her this morning way too much. She could get used to it.

She could start to love it.

So here they were in the hot baking sun outside a cave in the Lava Beds National Monument. The park was just south of the Oregon border and only an hour from their hotel. "I've never even heard of this place."

"Neither had I until I was looking for things to do up here on our trip." Grady was strapping on his bicycle helmet. He'd thought of everything. Instead of spelunking hats, or whatever cave dwellers called those things, he'd brought two bike helmets with him. He'd also equipped her with a high-powered flashlight and carried one himself.

He studied the map the ranger had given them. "We don't have to duckwalk or crawl through this one."

"Thank God." The last cave had narrowed to the point that she'd had to shuffle along like a duck. The narrower it got, the more claustrophobic she'd felt.

Entering the reserve, they'd crossed through a massive lava bed. Unlike Crater Lake, the park wasn't crowded. Landing at the ranger station, there'd been only three cars in the lot. They'd toured the exhibit room and learned that the caves were ancient lava tubes. Well, *she'd* learned that, because Grady already knew from his research, which was why he came prepared with flashlights and helmets. She had to admit how smart that was when she'd whacked her head on the low-slung ceiling of the first cave they'd entered. Without protection, she'd have been sporting a huge lump.

She wanted to ask if he'd ever done anything like this with his wife, but that would spoil the mood. Besides, she already knew. His wife would have hated it. That thought made Jordana even more willing to give it a shot. Whatever Grady wanted to show her, she was dying to see. They'd climbed down the Skull Cave's metal stairs until it was so cold, she'd started to shiver, especially compared to the heat up top. They'd duckwalked in the Valentine Cave, meeting only one couple on their way back out. And here in the Sentinel, there was no one. The longest of all the caves, it stretched from an upper entrance to a lower exit that came out partway down the hill, and was the only cave you didn't have to go back out the way you went in. Best of all, they didn't have to crawl. Jordana drew the line at crawling on her stomach.

"Ready?" Grady tugged her chin strap.

She swatted at him. "Yes." It was actually fascinating. In the early nineteen hundreds, people used to ice skate in one of the deepest caves. But warm air from below had melted the ice. She wondered if it was a sign of global warming.

Grady went first. According to the map, they would be able to walk upright the whole way. Trudging down beneath an arch that hadn't collapsed when the rest of the cave entrance opened up, they descended into the darkness. The deeper they went, the colder it got, but their flashlights drew a broad beam in front of them.

"There's the lava stream." Grady swirled his flashlight over the rock which had formed into swirls up the sides of the cave.

She was glad Grady had made her bring hiking boots. Rather than smooth walking paths, the cave floors were made of rock chunks and a spiky plaster-like material. In some places, the stones were sharp enough to slice right through athletic shoes.

"It's getting colder."

"You can have my jacket," he offered.

"No. Thanks. It's nice after being in the sun." The air grew mustier along the slow descent. In spots, the park rangers had installed metal stairs down dramatic drops and built bridges over chasms.

Leaning over the side of a metal railing, Jordana shone her light down. She couldn't see the bottom and when she dropped a pebble, she couldn't hear it land. There was nothing but endless darkness. "You sure wouldn't want to drop your flashlight down there," she said as they stepped off the bridge onto the rock path again.

"You wouldn't want to drop it anywhere in here."

She suppressed a shudder at the thought of being completely alone in the dark without her flashlight.

A step in front of her, Grady stopped. "Turn the light off," he told her. "Let's feel how really dark it is."

For just a moment, she wanted to say no. But that would be chicken. He switched his off first. Then she did.

It was beyond dark. Everything was completely black and oddly disorienting. She felt the lava walls creeping closer. The darkness was a physical thing she could sense along her limbs, raising the hairs on her arms, and beating against her chest.

If she dropped her flashlight now, she'd never find it. She'd never get out of here.

"It's so dark," she whispered, and the sound of her voice seemed to curl eerily around her, as if the darkness was trying to consume her.

Grady didn't answer. She couldn't even hear him breathe. For a panicked moment, she was terrified he'd disappeared like a magician and left her alone in here.

She was afraid to move, afraid even to shift the flashlight in her hand so she could switch it back on. God, what if she fumbled and dropped the lifeline?

"Grady?" Panic edged her voice. The dark was so disorienting, she almost felt as if she were falling. "Where are you?"

He reached out unerringly, his fingers touching her face, then cupping her cheek. "I'm right here. Right next to you. I won't leave you."

She only realized her heart had stopped when it stuttered to life again. It was as if he could actually find her in the dark, without a light, with nothing at all, as if he could see right into her soul. His strength washed over her, his presence filled her. And there in the dark with him, she wasn't afraid anymore. Grady was here, he'd never left her. He was steadfast, dependable, willing to do whatever was necessary. He was beside her all the way. She saw then that she truly had fallen, right into Grady, into everything he was as a man, as a human being. She didn't need the light to know he would never leave her alone.

Those moments in the cave set something off in Jordana. Her skin seemed to be humming, and she felt an answering thrum deep inside. Walking out of the cave behind Grady, she could concentrate on little else beyond the play of muscle in his shoulders, his back, his butt, his legs. He was all big, strong, perfect male. Her mouth watered with her desire. There was no explanation as to why his words in a dark cave could move her, but they did.

She wanted him. Now.

Driving out of the park, her fingers itched to touch him. She'd done naughty things in cars before, and she wanted to do them all with Grady, now, while he was driving, putting her hands on him, her lips, her mouth. Savoring him.

"Would you like to stop at the wildlife refuge?"

"No." He couldn't know that she was literally holding herself back in her seat so she didn't dive on him.

He glanced at her. "You sure? They have dragonflies with wings striped liked zebras out in these wetlands."

"No." Any other time, yes, but right now she didn't care one whit about zebra dragonflies. "I see you've been doing more research." She wanted him to research her, with his hands, his lips, his tongue, and every part of his body.

He laughed. "Party pooper."

She was on him in a moment, her hand cupping his sex. "Depends on the party we're talking about."

He sucked in a breath, and she felt him grow against her palm. "I'm all for that kind of party." A harsh note had crept into his voice.

"Then you better drive fast," she whispered.

She was on the other side of crazy when they finally arrived back at the hotel. The room had been cleaned, the bed made. And she wanted to mess it all up again. They tore off their clothes—he was definitely on the other side of crazy right along with her—then she pushed him down on the mattress, climbed on top, straddling his hips.

"Now what?" he asked, his eyes as dark as they'd been in the cave.

She felt his every hard ridge between her legs, and she pressed her advantage until he groaned. "I don't know," she told him. "But I think I need to taste every inch of you."

She wanted to lick him like an ice cream cone in Tahoe on a winter day, because it would take hours for him to melt, hours until she was down to the last drop.

He was right there. Right next to her. He wasn't leaving. She could savor him for as long as she wanted.

"Don't stop now." He surged up against her. "You're killing me."

Leaning down, she put her lips to his. "How long can you hold out?"

"For as long as you want me to."

A younger man would rush things, more about the end than the means, but Grady knew the pleasures of making it last.

She'd never had that. She was always rushing. With him, she wanted to slow down. She'd felt his unbridled desire, but now she wanted to relish the taste of his skin, his taut muscles, his salt, his sweet.

Stretching out on top of him, she savored his lips first, his tongue, stroking hers deep into his mouth. Then she licked his earlobes, drinking in his soft groans and faster breaths.

She'd always had sex before, but with Grady, it could almost be making love. His body against hers was poetry, the touch of their skin like music. Their temperatures rose together like the crescendo of a concerto. She slid down his body, kissing, licking, tasting, biting, savoring. With her teeth on his flat nipple, she discovered how sensitive he was when she nipped him lightly. He groaned, surged, grabbed her shoulders in his big hands, and his body trembled against her.

She felt so powerful, and yet so overwhelmed. She wanted him to let her do whatever she desired, yet needed him to beg.

She blew warm air on his wet nipple, and his shiver ran right through her. "Can you hold out?" she whispered the tease.

He tilted her chin up to meet his hot, dark gaze. "For however long you want."

Forever.

The word was frightening. Because forever didn't exist.

But she had this moment with him, and she wanted it to last a little longer. She kissed her way down his abdomen, tiny kisses that took the forever she craved. Just like he'd done to her this morning. Or last night. Or, oh God, all those beautiful, perfect times he'd touched her, put his mouth on her, driven her mad.

He was trembling by the time she cupped him in her hands and finally, after forever, slid all that sleek, hard, beautiful flesh between her lips. She sipped every drop that escaped. She relished every curve, every ridge, every vein. He pulsed with life, with desire, with need.

"Jesus," he whispered. "How do you do that to me?"

It was like his words in the cave, the same impact, seeping inside her, heating her, making her want and feel and need more in ways she never had with anyone else, not ever. More, more, more. Never enough.

Forever.

But nothing was forever.

She pulled back, almost abruptly, and said, "Now," her voice hard, rushed.

His chest rising and falling fast, hard, along with his breath, he was still able to say, "I can hold out as long you want me to."

She wanted him to hold out forever, wanted this moment to go on and on. Yet her need was so great, it terrified her.

"No," she told him. "I need it now. Right now." The condoms were just beyond her reach in the bedside drawer. She had to crawl away to grab one, and the loss of contact was an ache in her belly.

She grabbed a packet, almost tossed it at him, but when he had it on, he whispered, "Tell me what you want."

She wanted him to do her like he couldn't wait. And yet, God help her, she wanted him to twine his fingers through hers and slide slowly, deeply, sweetly inside her, his eyes on hers, seeing her, feeling her, only her.

As if they were making love.

She started to tremble.

"Co'mere." Desire slurred the words as he pulled her beneath him, his weight on her sweeter than anything.

Then he took her slowly, sweetly, deeply, his eyes locked on hers until she couldn't look at him anymore.

The feel of him was so good, better than anyone had ever been, like she was a part of him, like she'd been running on empty for so long that she hadn't a clue how badly she needed him to fill her up.

With every slow thrust of his body, another empty space inside her took its fill of him. Then he was moving faster, higher, reaching the hollow around her heart and filling that, too.

The orgasm rolled over her so suddenly it was like an avalanche. It was like turning the flashlight off in the cave and feeling his hand on her, hearing his voice against her ear. Momentous. Overwhelming. Dragging her under. She rocked and tumbled with him, crying out his name. She held him so tight, her arms hurt and her legs ached, but she couldn't let go.

It felt like communion. It felt like their souls touched.

It felt like making love.

CHAPTER NINETEEN

Their three days and two nights were idyllic, a fantasy, a daydream. Grady made love to Jordana when they returned from the caves, and later, just before they fell asleep in each other's arms, then again in the middle of the night and once more the next morning. They didn't even leave the room, just ordered in, feeding each other on the big bed, drinking champagne in the huge tub, soaking in its heat, *their* heat. They'd had breakfast in bed and feasted on each other as well. Nothing had ever been so sweet.

The fantasy died when he dropped her off at her apartment Monday evening. Jordana hadn't ask him in. She'd kissed him on the cheek and whispered in his ear. *A-plus, Mr. Masterson.*

Then she was gone.

It was as if a door had opened, then slammed shut right in his face.

Driving away from her, he'd felt something tear loose inside him, like a tiny hole in his gut that would grow until finally everything would gush out of him. To Jordana, their trip had been nothing more than another of her role-plays, pretending they were lovers. She didn't want a man stealing her independence. She didn't want a relationship that would get in the way of her career. She liked to eat her slice of chocolate cake, then move on to red velvet or rum cake. She didn't want too much of any one thing. She didn't want to *need* only one kind of cake.

It was worse on Tuesday morning. Answering questions for Ivy on her new HR role, Jordana smiled at him like always. The hole in his gut ripped wider. A few drops of his blood seeped out. His heart felt the loss even as he smiled right back at her. As if they had a secret that would always be clandestine, that it was only temporary.

And why would it be anything else? Jordana had taught him everything he needed to know to get his wife back. Class over, graduation day.

After an excruciatingly long staff meeting, he closed his office door and shut everything out. In the quiet, the answer suddenly seemed so simple. His heart ached in a way it hadn't when he'd read Darlene's email. Even at the time, his emotion hadn't been grief or loss; it was anger. It was still anger. The only way to excise the wound was to lance it. Darlene didn't want him. She'd found another man. She'd started a new life. He wanted his own chance at a new life.

And he wanted it with Jordana.

She'd taught him more than what a woman wanted. She'd shown him what *he* wanted, revealed everything he'd been missing. And he'd *never* had any of that with Darlene. He'd been complacent, living in his comfortable routines, having sex like clockwork. No wonder Darlene had been searching for something else. No wonder she'd left him.

He'd taken their life together for granted.

He would not be complacent anymore. He couldn't predict what Jordana would do. He couldn't force her to change how she conducted her relationships. But he found one ray of hope in something she'd told him. She didn't rule out marriage because someday she might want a child. Which meant that someday she would consider a relationship with the right man.

Someday was here. And he was the right man. But she might never know that if he didn't tell her what he wanted.

But first he had to deal with his marriage.

Ivy had called Jordana over to her desk three times today. The issues weren't difficult, but Jordana had to admit she'd set up her computer filing system in a way that made perfect sense to her but wasn't completely intuitive to anyone else. Though that was a good tactic against someone who'd hacked her files, with Ivy taking over, she needed to do some documentation.

The real problem wasn't Ivy. The problem was Jordana herself. She could have answered the questions over the phone, but no, she had to walk over and demonstrate. And why? Pathetically, she'd wanted a glimpse of Grady.

His desk lay between them, his twenty-five-inch computer monitor cutting his face in half. He moved his mouse in his strong hand, touching it, stroking it, caressing it…

Oh God. She should have been able to let go. He'd passed all his lessons with enough gold stars to cover every inch of her naked body, *naked body* being the operative description. She wasn't done with him. She couldn't stop thinking about him. Everything had been so much worse—and so much better—after that moment in the cave. She'd felt a connection, something binding them together. It was beyond lust, beyond sex, beyond everything, and it came out in the way he'd touched her in the cave, in her kisses later that afternoon and in the night, and how solid his arms felt around her as they'd slept. Yesterday when he'd dropped her off, she'd wanted to beg on her hands and knees, preferably with her mouth on him, too.

She'd never had three days like that. She'd never felt cherished for three whole days. She wasn't done with the fantasy of having him and keeping him. She wanted to beg him to play the game with her a little longer.

But *she* hadn't begged. She hadn't said anything except that he'd passed all his classes with gold stars. She couldn't have said another word, because it meant that everything between them was over and he'd be going back to *her*.

She did not—no-no-no-no-no—want to think about Grady doing all *their* things with that woman. She didn't want to imagine his sexts or his dirty phone calls, or his hands, his lips, and his tongue all over some other woman's body. Some *other* woman. And there was the big issue. *Jordana* was the other woman.

Grady had to go back sometime. That had always been the basis for everything they'd done.

"So." Ivy tucked her short, dark hair behind her ear

and smiled sweetly. She probably smiled like that when her daughter was being a pill, too. "You've got all the files set up by department? What if I know a name and can't remember the department number?"

Jordana chewed on her bottom lip so she didn't shriek. Ivy's question was completely reasonable. Jordana was the unreasonable one, her fingers curling into talons because Ivy was diverting her attention away from Grady.

The desk phone rang. Ivy held up a finger. "Human Resources," she said so politely the sugar-coating in her voice could crack. Then her eyes widened. "Oh." She glanced at Jordana, then into Grady's office. "Hold on a minute, let me check." She punched a hold button and slapped the receiver to her chest. "It's Grady's *wife* downstairs in the lobby," she whispered loudly. "She's *never* come here."

Jordana's insides dropped like the wrong half of a weighted scale. Grady's wife was on the up side, and she was on the down, way down.

"Tell the receptionist to give her a guest badge and send her up," Grady called.

Bending over Ivy's desk to look at the monitor, her spine suddenly locked in place. She couldn't move, couldn't look at Grady, couldn't run away.

He hadn't even waited twenty-four hours to call his wife. No, he'd probably dropped Jordana off—after their fabulously sexy weekend—then immediately gotten on his cell and begged his wife for a discussion about their problems. Hah, he'd probably had to leave her a damn message because she never answered if she saw his name on the ID. Then he'd waited with bated breath until finally she deigned to call him back.

God help her, she sounded so vicious. But her insides felt like Grady had shoved them through the shredder. She was only vaguely aware of Ivy speaking into the phone as she prayed that Grady would *not* come out of his office. Wait, wait, it would be better if he *did* come out, if he went down there to meet his wife so Jordana wouldn't have to see her.

God, oh, God, she had to get out of here, run to her office, slam the door. Hide. She couldn't bear to see the woman. What if Grady touched his wife, grabbed her, hugged her? Oh my God, what if he actually *kissed* her? Jordana would die, absolutely *die*.

"She'll be right up, Grady," Ivy called as if she didn't see the fissures cracking Jordana's façade. "Okay, so," she said in a normal tone, "you were saying about the department numbers?"

What on earth was Ivy talking about?

Oh, yeah, the files. Jordana could finish this in two seconds, then skitter off around the opposite end of the cubicles and get to her office without having to see... that... *bitch!*

"Okay, this is how I do it." She rattled off instructions which she wasn't sure even made sense. The only thing she could think about was what Grady's wife would say when he told her he'd finally figured out what she wanted, that he was a changed man, that he could fix everything.

"I'm not quite getting it," Ivy said with a sweet smile that meant Jordana was no longer speaking in coherent sentences.

"Why don't I come back later?" Her mind was all jumbled.

"Well, I do need to pull this together for Rhonda pretty quick."

Screw Rhonda. She did not shriek. Then she heard the outer door open and close.

"If you just show me this one thing," Ivy was saying.

It was too late. The woman rounded the cubicle corner and headed straight for them. She was sophisticated in a tailored, black-and-white business suit, the skirt well above the knee and her high heels a mile tall. Her auburn hair was thick and silky, her makeup accentuating her eyes and lips. She was perfect. She was more than Jordana could ever hope to be. Everything Grady could possibly want.

Jordana felt her heart being sliced and diced in Grady's shredder.

"You can go right in," Ivy pointed to Grady's open door, then whispered under her breath, "Wow."

Wow was right. Maybe Grady couldn't change her mind. Maybe she was already planning her move into the other guy's house. Maybe she was here only to hand him the divorce papers.

Jordana's mind tripped over itself with all the scenarios rushing through it.

But her heart knew there was no maybe about it. Grady would say whatever was necessary to change his wife's mind. He'd make her see the other guy was just some lust buddy. He wasn't long-term. He was just the foreman who told her he dreamed about her, the engineer who dragged her into the ladies' room, the guy who put her hand between his legs to warm her up. None of them were Grady. And the wandering wife would see the light, admit how stupid she'd been, throw herself into his arms, begging forgiveness and spewing undying love.

Jordana didn't hear Grady's voice. She only heard the click of the door as it shut her out.

In a cowardly act—and she hated admitting to her cowardice, but there it was—Jordana hid out in her office as the day waned, the shadows moving across her desk, and her computer clock counting down each successive minute. People cleared out for the evening, and the silence grew heavy.

She told herself it didn't hurt, that she wasn't *losing* Grady. She'd never had him in the first place. He was always going back to his wife. She'd known it. She'd helped him figure out how to do it. It was just that…

She gulped air. She was not going to cry. She didn't cry over men. She hadn't cried when Eddie left her for his wife. She couldn't even remember crying when her dad ran away from her, but she was only three at the time. Yes, she'd been hurt, and okay, she was hurting now. She'd gotten her emotions involved.

She closed her eyes, remembering those moments in the pitch dark of that cave.

I'm right here. Right next to you. I won't leave you.

Grady's voice had soothed her. His touch had felt momentous. And she'd let herself get carried away.

But it wasn't real. His wife was real. It was better that he went back to her. In a few short weeks, Jordana would want to move on anyway. She always had, and she always would. They didn't have a future. They *couldn't* have one.

She wasn't built that way. She was temporary.

If only it would stop hurting.

I won't leave you.

He'd said it as if he would *always* be there. And in his arms, she'd actually wanted him *always* to be there. She'd let herself feel as if they were making love.

She should never have done that. After that moment in the cave, when she'd felt so connected to him, a part of him, she should have made him drive her all the way back home right then.

Her desk phone rang, and she nearly shrieked. She'd thought she was alone in the building, everyone gone. Even Grady, she was sure, had left with his wife.

She picked up. "Hello?" She sounded ridiculously timid, as if her raw emotions were hanging out.

"Meet me in the conference room. Now." Grady's deep voice thrummed with authority.

The timbre of it stroked her nerve endings, setting them on fire.

Why hadn't he followed his wife? Maybe he'd felt obligated to tell Jordana that their plan had worked. What if he wanted to celebrate? She would absolutely die.

Don't make me do this. That's what she wanted to beg. But she could get through this. It was the best thing for Grady, and honestly it was best for her, too. She was too attached. And she'd never allowed herself any attachments before.

He was already there when she arrived, leaning against the big oak table. Her heart seized. He was more beautiful than any man had a right to be.

I'm right here. Right next to you. I won't leave you.

But he *was* leaving.

"How did it go?" she asked, sounding so utterly normal that she shocked herself. She came to stand close to him, too close, but she knew it would be the last time.

"She was full of surprises," he said with a quirk of his lips.

Her stomach was churning like a washing machine, but his scent was all over her, inside her. "And what would those be?"

"She's been rethinking our situation."

Okay, now her stomach was more like a dryer drum going round and round, everything beating against the sides as if she'd thrown her tennis shoes in there. She was shaky with the need to touch him. "And of course she realizes she made a mistake. We already knew that."

He laughed. She adored his laughter, how it filled his face and reached his beautiful eyes. "What about using all the techniques you taught me?"

She stretched her lips in a caricature of a smile. "Keep them in reserves."

"I won't need to." His eyes were deep, dark chocolate.

The drum just went around and around until she felt sick. "Getting cocky now?"

"Never." He shook his head, just one way and the other, then he stopped. "I will never take what I have for granted again. You taught me that."

God. She didn't want to have taught him anything that would help keep that woman in his life. "I'm so glad I could help." Did that sound snarky? No. She sounded normal, thank God.

"You're not getting the picture." He crossed his arms over the gorgeous chest she'd laid her head on.

"I'm definitely not missing it." Again, she surprised herself with the dry, even tone.

He stood then, and she felt his towering height right down in her bones. She loved his height, loved how his big body made her feel surrounded, possessed, cherished.

"I learned what *you* desire," he said so softly that the hairs on her arms rose to attention. "And I found I don't care what Darlene wants."

Darlene. He usually said *my wife.* Jordana hated hearing her name now.

She couldn't let him know how it affected her. "Of course you care what she wants. That's why we did all this. So you could get her back."

He put one finger beneath her chin and lifted. "You're not a stupid woman. You know what I'm saying."

"No," she whispered. "I don't." But God, she could pray.

CHAPTER TWENTY

Grady remembered every word of that conversation, every nuance of Darlene's body language. And he recalled his emotions, even the lack of them.

In that first moment, he'd had no idea why Darlene had come. He'd told her he wanted to meet after office hours at the same bar they'd gone to almost three weeks ago, the night she'd told him she thought about other men when she was in bed with him.

Maybe she wanted to humiliate him just a little bit more or get something extra out of the divorce settlement.

Whatever, she'd arrived. And Grady had resorted to his usual politeness.

"Have a seat." He pointed to the small conference table in the corner of his office. He didn't want to sit at his desk and see Jordana through the glass partition at the side of the door. She was too distracting, reminding him of every moment of their weekend, every touch, every kiss. And with Darlene, he needed his wits.

Darlene pulled out the chair and sat, crossing her legs

with an elegant swish. She didn't bother to pull the skirt back down as it rode higher on her thighs.

"Grady, sweetheart, we need to talk." She used her nut-cracking, sensual voice.

He didn't feel much of anything, not even anger. It was as if he could sit back and watch her like she was a pretty but shallow woman sitting across from him in the doctor's office right before he had to go in for a prostate exam.

"I don't want the house," he said. "You can buy me out. Or we can sell it and split the proceeds." They'd purchased it a couple of years before the mortgage crisis so they didn't stand to make much profit.

She breathed deeply, her breasts expanding the fitted jacket. "I don't want to live in that house alone, Grady."

"Then we'll sell."

Putting her elbows on the armrests, she laced her fingers. "Grady," she said softly, and he knew that voice. She wanted something, probably custody of the new seventy-eight-inch curved TV.

He wondered why he was being so harsh when he professed to having lost his anger. And then he knew. He just wanted it to be over. He didn't want to fight, but he didn't want to be complacent either.

"You can buy me out on the TV, too." He wasn't so sure he liked curved anymore. You had to be at just the right angle to enjoy it at its best. Somehow that seemed to be a metaphor for his marriage, too.

She leaned forward then, huffing at him. "I don't want the TV."

"Then I'll buy you out."

Her lips pursed. "Grady, will you listen to me?"

"You haven't said anything yet."

"That's because you aren't giving me a chance."

"Then here's your chance to tell me what you want." He knew what Jordana wanted. He knew how to make her beg. He knew how to show her that he desired her, that he couldn't keep his hands off her, that he couldn't get her out of his head.

But he still didn't know what Darlene wanted. And even if he did, he no longer had the desire to give it to her.

"I made a mistake." She flexed her fingers, examining her nails for a moment as if she'd just had her manicure done.

He wasn't sure he was hearing correctly. "A mistake about what?"

She clucked her tongue. "Why are you making this so hard?"

"Making what so hard?"

She breathed sharply in, then out. "You want me to pay. You want to see me beg. You want me to tell you what a fool I was."

Finally, he got it. Because really, he wasn't stupid. "Are you saying you want to come back?"

She wheezed out a "*Yes*." Her lips pressed together, then she added. "I was wrong. I was looking for something." She waved her hand in the air as if she could grab whatever it was. "I guess it was excitement. I wanted to feel like a woman again."

"You wanted to feel desired," he added for her.

She lost all her affectation. "Yes. That's what I wanted."

Grady knew the answer. "And he made you feel that way."

She looked down. "For a little while. Then I realized he wasn't what I thought he was." She sniffed and looked up. "He wasn't you."

Grady didn't laugh, although he could have. "So when the excitement and lust wore off, there wasn't anything left."

"Exactly." There was just an ounce of awe in her voice, as if she couldn't believe he'd understand so quickly or easily. "For a while, I felt like a woman. I didn't feel like I was past forty and on the downhill slide. But I mistook the lust for what I feel for you."

"And what is that?" Maybe it was cruel to make her continue. He didn't want her to beg.

"Love, Grady. You know it's love."

Actually, he didn't know that. And he was pretty sure that Darlene didn't either. She hadn't woken up to the fact that she loved him. She'd woken up to the fact that she *didn't* love Mr. GQ. And that Mr. GQ didn't have Grady's income. Together he and Darlene had moved long past love into complacency. They had a good life, a nice home, new cars every couple of years, the latest gadgets and toys. And that had been enough. It probably would still be enough if he hadn't asked Jordana what women really wanted.

And now it would never be enough. Jordana had given him a taste of everything he could ever desire. He wasn't willing to settle for comfortable anymore.

He wasn't willing to settle for his old life with Darlene or a woman who dreamed of someone else when he made love to her. He would *never* let Jordana think about another man. He would make sure he was the only one. And she'd taught him exactly how to do that. He wanted whatever he could have with her, as much or as little as she would give him to start. And then he would fight for the rest.

"I don't want this to sound cruel," he said softly.

Darlene opened her mouth, and the flicker of fear moistened her eyes. "Grady."

His name on her lips couldn't stop him. "It's too late."

"It's only been a month." She swallowed, all her self-confidence sliding down her throat.

"It's exactly thirty-three days too late."

She shook her head slightly. "But he really didn't mean a thing."

She didn't understand that Mr. GQ meant everything. He was the writing on the wall. He was the eye-opener. He was the end. "He doesn't matter."

"But Grady, our life, everything we had, we can't just throw it away."

He could have said she was the one who'd thrown it away. "I don't want that anymore. You were right. I was comfortable. I had my routine. I was complacent. You taught me that." And Jordana had taught him everything else. "Let's just move on."

"If you want to move on, why are you still wearing your wedding ring?" She pointed one beautifully red-tipped fingernail.

He glanced down, remembering his thought that night at the bar when the young woman hit on him. When his desire for Jordana had completely seduced him. The ring was an appendage. And wearing it was a way not to deal with life changes. "It's just a ring."

Something flashed in her eyes, maybe it was pain,

maybe it was anger. But she didn't give up. "I can make it better, Grady. I can try harder."

He didn't feel any victory in finally making Darlene be the one who begged. "Shh," he whispered. "Don't."

She went still, breathing softly a few moments. Until finally she said, "You're right. I'm belittling myself." She gathered her purse to her chest and stood, smoothing her skirt down as far as it would go. "You can buy out the TV. I don't like the curve anyway." Obviously neither of them had.

Then she left him for the second and final time.

A month ago, Darlene's departure had devastated and enraged him. Today, he had to thank her. She'd helped him find Jordana. She'd provided the means for him to unearth the aliveness he hadn't even known he was missing. He'd discovered it with Jordana. He'd discovered intense desire. Jordana had once said that you couldn't have love without first having lust. Well, he sure as hell felt both now, deeply, in his bones, his DNA, his heart, all for her. And he didn't intend to be one of her temporary friends with benefits.

She had taught him how to live. He would teach her how to love.

Her heart beating like a bunny rabbit suddenly seeing the bobcat looming right over her, Jordana waited for Grady to say something. Anything. *Everything.*

"Let me explain," he said so softly it was like the stroke of his finger over her cheek. "I don't care that

Darlene has realized she was only in lust with the other guy or that his bank account wasn't as big as some of his other attributes. She wanted a divorce, and she can have it. I'm not going to spend the rest of my life doing my emails while we're sitting in front of the TV, or having sex like clockwork on Saturday nights."

Her breath hitched in her chest. "Only on Saturdays?"

He was so close, she could smell his unique male scent, musky, sexy, spicy. She breathed it in like a vapor cure.

"I want it every day. Every morning, every night. Whenever I can get it. With you. No one else." He gave a very slight shake of his head. "*That's* what you taught me. How to please *you*. How to go crazy for *you*." Leaning in, his voice whispered across her hair. "How to make *you* crazy."

Her fingers were tingling, her body all jittery. She trembled as if she'd just downed a whole glass of champagne and the bubbles had fizzed her brain. "It's only been a month."

He laughed softly. "That's what Darlene said. Sometimes that's all it takes to realize you've been running on empty without even knowing it."

This wasn't right. It couldn't be true. She was fantasizing in a dream world. "This is just some sort of rebound thing." She tried to explain it away. "It's lust that hasn't worn off yet."

"No." His voice shivered through her. "I know what I had, and I know what this is." He twisted the wedding ring off his finger and held it in the palm of his hand.

Through everything they'd done, even the glorious

weekend in Oregon, he'd never taken off that ring. All Jordana could do was stare at it.

"I've been hiding behind this ring, hiding behind the sex we've had as if it was all just another lesson. But it stopped being a lesson long ago." He closed his hand around the ring and shoved it in his pocket. "It was making love, Jordana. I love you."

Love. Oh God. He loved her. Her heart wanted to burst wide open, yet she'd learned a long, long time ago that men didn't mean it. At least not permanently. "But Grady, you know I'm only short-term."

"You just never found the right man."

She wanted to step into him, press her body against his, put her lips to his throat and lick his salty-sweet skin. But she knew herself and she knew men. The thought of him with his wife made her want to lose her stomach all over her shoes, but she'd get over it. Just like she'd gotten over Eddie. And her father.

She backed away. "It would never work."

"Why not?" He sounded so sure, as if he knew she didn't have an answer.

"Because."

He was right there, filling her whole gaze. "*Because* isn't good enough."

"Things always end," she managed.

"They don't have to." His breath warmed her cheek.

She had to insist. "But they do."

He tilted his head slightly to the side and held her gaze unblinkingly until she was forced to look down. "You're afraid to try," he said so softly that she trembled.

"I'm not *afraid*." She didn't like the word. "I just know myself."

"You're afraid I'll change my mind and chose my wife over you just like your best friend did."

She felt her ribcage tightening around her heart like a vise. Eddie didn't count in this. Not at all. "I am not." While Grady had been closeted in his office with his wife, Jordana hadn't been afraid. She was hurt, that was all, and she'd get over it.

"I'm not changing my mind. Not about her. And not about you." If only he wasn't so close that she could breathe him right into her lungs.

If only she could manage one step back. "Grady, you can't know that. And anyway, that's not the point. I don't do relationships."

"You said you don't do them now because of your career. But I'm not going to interfere with your career."

She spread her hands as if she could ward him off. It would hurt so much less now than it would later when he decided to go back to his wife. He might have taken off his wedding ring for the first time, but that didn't mean he would never put it back on. "Please, you've got to understand."

"I understand perfectly."

He was so calm, so freaking reasonable, that it made her *totally* unreasonable. "You *don't* understand," she said through gritted teeth.

"You like quick and dirty so that you don't get attached and you don't get hurt when it's over."

Her body chilled, and her skin turned clammy. "I don't get attached and I don't get hurt."

"Do you remember what I said in the cave?"

I'm right here. Right next to you. I won't leave you. "I have no idea what you're talking about."

"I said I won't leave you."

She *tsk*ed as if that had meant nothing. "We were talking about being in the dark."

"I wasn't talking about the dark. I was talking about us. I made love to you all weekend and called my ex-wife when we got back to tell her I agree to the divorce."

The heels of her shoes felt like they'd grown right down into the floor, nailing her to the spot. "You called her to tell her that?"

"Yes. She surprised me with her change of tune. But that didn't make any difference to what I'd decided or how I feel."

He'd chosen her over his wife.

He was right there, forcing her to look up, forcing her to *see* him when he said so very softly, "Don't throw me away like all the others."

"I didn't—"

He put his fingers over her lips. "You did. And I understand that you're afraid. But I'm not leaving."

How many times could she deny that she'd been terrified he was going back to his wife? She'd sat in her office with her heart and her insides feeling like they were spilling out all over the carpet.

But Grady wasn't stopping. "I'm not like your best friend. I'm not like your foreman or your engineer. I'm not walking away and I'm not giving up. Because I know you have feelings for me. I'm not going to be some complacent guy who doesn't push you to admit what you feel. You said you could have loved your best friend. I'm not going to let you decide when it's too late that you *could* have loved me."

Eddie had given in to his wife's demands and stopped

being Jordana's friend. But how many chances did they have before that? Why had she only realized she *could* have loved him when it was too late? When he'd already left?

"I'm not like all the other men in your life."

Grady was smart. He had integrity. He made her laugh. He admitted when he was wrong. He was willing to change. And he stood up for what he believed in.

He would never walk out on his best friend. He would never walk out on his kid.

But how many people had she walked out on?

"Do you really think I'm afraid?" Her voice was less than a whisper. "That it's all because I'm afraid?" She'd never wanted to even think it.

He cupped her face in his hands, his lips only a kiss away. "You don't have to be afraid with me. I will never drop the flashlight in the dark."

She laughed, but it was almost a hiccup. "What do you really want, Grady?"

"Everything." The word was a harsh exclamation, then he hauled her high in his arms and shoved her up against the conference room wall. "I want *you.*

He devoured her with his mouth, pushing past her lips, delving deep inside, all the way to her heart. She raised her legs to his waist and clutched him close, steadying herself against him. He kissed her until she couldn't breathe and had to pull back to drag in gasps of air.

"I'll always want you and love you this way," he murmured into her hair. "So badly my guts feel like they're tied up in knots."

She'd always gone for the fast and furious because she knew it couldn't last. She'd left her lovers before they could leave her. She'd said it was to protect her career, but maybe it was just to protect her heart. She'd left L.A. and walked away from Eddie, never even given him a chance, never given *herself* the chance. She'd let him fall for someone else. But would she survive if Grady left?

"What if I'm a failure at a relationship?" She whispered her fears softly against his throat.

"I won't let you fail. I won't let either of us fail." He leaned back, his smile turning her heart to mush.

She wrapped her arms around him, pressing herself tight to his chest. She would *never* survive. She would live with regret for the rest of her life. And that was worse than failure. "I love you, Grady. I've been afraid to put a name to what you make me feel, but that's what it is."

"I know it is. Because I know exactly what a woman wants."

God, how she loved his cocky smile. "You know exactly what *I* want and don't you go practicing my techniques with anyone else."

He lowered his voice to total sincerity. "Never."

She kissed him with everything she had, heart, body, and soul. Everything except the fear she'd allowed to rule her life for so many years. Now she would only let love rule her heart. Well, actually, she'd let desire rule, too. She was, after all, a desire junkie, and where Grady was concerned, she always would be.

Then she gasped. "Oh my God, we're going to have to tell Rhonda about our relationship." A *real* relationship.

"And Brett." He slid his hand beneath her hair, cupping her nape. "Baby, we'll have to go public. Can you handle that?"

She'd lived her love life in secret. But Grady was bringing her out of the shadows. "Yes," she whispered.

"Just don't drop the flashlight."

"Not a chance. Because I love you." Then he kissed her like it was a vow.

With Grady, she would never have to be afraid of love again.

The End

So… what really happened between Gloria and Parker Hunt?
Look for their story in **Love Affair to Remember**, Book 2 in the *After Office Series*. Coming soon

ABOUT THE AUTHOR

NY Times and USA Today bestselling author Jennifer Skully is a lover of contemporary romance, bringing you poignant tales peopled with hilarious characters that will make you laugh and make you cry. Look for Jennifer's new series written with Bella Andre, starting with *Breathless in Love*, The Maverick Billionaires Book 1. Writing as Jasmine Haynes, she's authored over 35 classy, sensual romance tales about real issues such as growing older, facing divorce, starting over. Her books have passion and heart and humor and happy endings, even if they aren't always traditional. She also writes gritty, paranormal mysteries in the Max Starr series. Having penned stories since the moment she learned to write, she now lives in the Redwoods of Northern California with her husband and their adorable nuisance of a cat who totally runs the household.

Connect with Jennifer Skully & Jasmine Haynes

Newsletter signup: http://bit.ly/SkullyNews
Jennifer's Website: www.jenniferskully.com
Blog: www.jasminehaynes.blogspot.com
Facebook: www.facebook.com/jasminehaynesauthor
Twitter: https://twitter.com/jasminehaynes1

Printed in Great Britain
by Amazon

77190713R00167